PAUL

THE

RECKLESS

OR THE

FUGITIVES DOOM

PAUL THE RECKLESS;

OR,

THE FUGITIVE'S DOOM.

CHAPTER I.

" You tremble, Florence, as if apprehensive of some hidden danger ! Do you then deem my arm so weak that I cannot protect her who, by this interview, has afforded me another proof of her confidence and love ?"

These words were spoken by a young man to a fair and beautiful girl, who, pale and agitated, leant on his arm for support as they slowly wended their way through a sequestered spot, which superstition, for time out of mind, had designated under the somewhat startling appellation of " The Haunted Hollow." For a few moments the maiden returned no answer, but at last recalling to her mind the words that had been uttered, she made an effort to regain some of her composure, and with still faltering accents, replied :—

" I do indeed tremble, yet is it more for your danger than any that may threaten myself. At this early hour in the morning I have ventured to secretly quit the house of my father, but, should a discovery take place, I fear the consequences will be even more terrible than those my fears have conjured up in my mind."

" Dearest Florence," exclaimed her lover, " if anything could have increased my love, it is the constancy of the affection with which you regard me,—the endurance of your love, though circumstances have occurred that impute to me a career of guilt. I will freely confess to you that I have thoughtlessly suffered myself to be drawn into the vortex of folly, yet, while I do so, you must not be offended with me for saying that your father has been scarcely less free from blame than myself. He has not escaped crime, and, therefore, should not be too severe against one who has at least the palliative of inexperience to plead in his own favour."

" I have never listened to your traducers," she replied, " because I have always believed your love to be as sincere as my own, and even parental authority has failed to make me false to the vows I have uttered."

" Your words inspire me with renewed hopes," exclaimed the other, " and I can now laugh at the treacherous sneers of a world that I have learnt to despise. Truly has it been said that I have led a wild and reckless life, but it is never too late to retrieve our errors, and with such an example as you constantly before me, there will be every motive to regain the world's respect, which had well nigh been lost for ever. Nay, the excesses of which your father now complains were occasioned by his own evil advice and example, though he would set himself up as the censor of morality."

" Yet," cried Florence, " you may well excuse the anxiety of a parent, who regards the welfare of his daughter beyond all other earthly things."

" He knows I love you," returned the other, " and how could he expect otherwise, when, through his own means, I have been thrown so much in your society? He first allows a strong feeling of regard to spring up between us, and would then crush the very hopes that he has himself given birth to."

" You are too severe in your censures upon my father," exclaimed the maiden. " If he has faults, it is not for his child to rise up against him as a judge, and, once for all, I again declare that nothing shall ever make me false to the vows I have uttered. Our meetings shall take place in this lonely spot as usual, for superstition has rendered it nearly deserted, except by the wandering tribes of gipsies who occasionally seek the shelter it affords."

" The place is not quite so secret as you imagine," replied her lover, " for whilst I was waiting for you just now, I saw old Beaumont, of the Manor House, with his friend, Stephen Harland, taking their early walk in this direction. The old fellow has quarrelled with almost all the world, and should he chance to see us together, there's no saying what mischief he may spread abroad."

As he finished speaking he directed the attention of Florence to an opening amongst the trees where the very persons he was speaking of were seen passing along on their way.

" They are still lingering about, I see," he exclaimed, " yet I am in hopes they are so engaged in conversation that they have not observed us. Again they have disappeared, dear Florence, and we must now part lest this interview of ours should be discovered by others who would not fail to make the most of it. Ere we take leave of each other, however, let us vow that no circumstances shall ever prevent the union we have projected. Say, love, will you pledge yourself to remain true and constant to me for ever?"

" I do," she solemnly replied ; " I will be yours, or pass my life in celibacy for your sake. They may speak ill of you, but my ears shall ever be deaf to their foul slanders ; and when all difficulties are removed, I will freely and joyfully give you my hand."

"Thanks—a thousand thanks, dear girl," he joyfully exclaimed. "I was wrong, perhaps, to ask for a vow, and yet the love I bear you, and the fears I entertain of loving you, would scarcely be satisfied with less. From this time I will endeavour to gain the approbation of my fellow men, and prove myself worthy of the prize it has been my fondest object to obtain. I will rely upon you, Florence, but, should you ever prove false to your promise, madness will so far overcome me, that I may even resort to violence rather than lose her upon whom my every hope of happiness depends."

"You do but injure me by such a thought," answered Florence, "for no consideration shall ever make me false to the promise I have solemnly given. Nay, may a withering curse fall upon those who would endeavour to blight the fair hopes of joy that we have fondly believed one day will be ours."

"None will dare to interpose when it is known that my resolution is formed," exclaimed the other. "But, hush! I hear footsteps approaching, and we must now part, lest we should be discovered together. Farewell, dear girl, and fail not to meet me at this spot as often as opportunity will admit."

Having given utterance to these hasty words, he sprang into a thicket, and scarcely had he disappeared than a gipsy woman approached the place where Florence was standing, and dropping a low courtesy, she exclaimed, in a whining tone,—

"A fair good day to you, my young lady. Aha! this is a fine place for lovers to meet in ; though, perhaps, 'tis scarcely prudent to trust yourself with him who has just gone way. If you would know your fortune, miss, cross my palm with a piece of money, and you shall hear something that may be of service. Nay, you seem to doubt me ; but to prove that I make no vain boast, I will tell you the very words that passed but just now between you and your lover."

"You have been listening, then!" said Florence, in accents of alarm.

"Indeed I have not, young lady," answered the gipsy ; "yet can I tell you as truly all that has passed as if I had heard every word uttered by him that has gone away."

Florence remained for some few minutes silent and doubtful, but being again appealed to by the woman, she slipped a piece of money into her hand, and was turning away, when the other demanded if she would not hear that which she had to tell.

"What," asked Florence, "can you tell me that I may already anticipate?"

"More than a guileless soul like yours may willingly believe," answered the woman. "He who has but now left you is a serpent against whose wiles I would caution you to beware. Banish him from your heart, and see him no more, or there will be sorrow, and repentance, and death!"

"Your prediction is a false one," cried Florence, indignantly ; "for he whom I love is worthy the regard with which he has inspired me. I have known him, watched him, and never has he, by word or action, betrayed a symptom of the base treachery with which your words accuse him."

"This over confidence will prove your destruction," exclaimed the gipsy, with increasing earnestness. "The warning you have heard is given by a friend that is watchful in your behalf, and who would save you from the ruin and despair that must be the consequence of this designing man's pretended love."

"Say rather," said Florence, "that it is given by one who has some vengeful motive of her own to serve. I know him to be the very soul of honour ; yet would you prejudice me against him, by words that you have no means of proving."

"The proof will come soon enough, if you heed me not," returned the old woman. "I warn you against the foul practices of an artful villain, that you may secure the happiness which it is still in your power to obtain."

"How is it to be done?"

" By giving your hand to one who deserves the love he now begins to de-spair of."

" Your words are incomprehensible," exclaimed Florence ; " of whom do you speak ?"

" His name may not be uttered," replied the gipsy ; " but it will not be diffi-cult to guess the person I allude to.   Pause, then, ere you consent to become the bride of sorrow, and, little as you seem to heed the words I utter, lay them up in your heart, and the evil I warn you against may be averted."

" There is some motive in all this that I cannot at present discover," exclaimed Florence.   " You have spoken shame of one who merits, and has gained my love, yet no proof have you given me that there is any foundation for so heavy a charge."

" If I have succeeded in bringing your mind to reflection, my task is more than half done," returned the other.   " I will now leave you to weigh my words, and my parting caution is that you will at least believe me honest in the warn-ing I have given.   Farewell, Florence Campell ! and when next you see me, let it be to say that you have banished from your heart the love of him who seeks to brings you to destruction."

Florence turned her steps homewards, and the old woman had scarcely re-sumed her own way through the hollow when she was met by another person, to whom she addressed herself in the usual whining accents with which she plied her trade.

" Good morrow to you, Master Richard Elliot," she exclaimed ; " you have left your bed betimes this morning, and that, I take it, is a sign there is business of importance a-foot.   Nay, turn not so proudly from me, but rather stay and have your fortune told, which I promise you shall not be a bad one."

" You old hag !" muttered Elliot, sullenly, " if you do not let a gentleman pass on his way I can tell your fortune, which I promise you will not be a very good one."

" You threaten me ?"

" Ay, with the horse-pond, unless you take care of what you are about."

" You are out of temper this morning," exclaimed the gipsy ; " but for all that you would not injure a poor old woman that never did you harm."

" That will depend upon yourself," he replied ; " yet tell me, you have been to the Manor-house, I think, and have seen a certain pretty lass there that I am rather taken with ?"

" Your honour means Patty, the dairy-maid ?"

" The same."

" And have told her her fortune ?"

" I have," replied the gipsy ; " and your honour was not forgotten when I told her what a fine lady she is to be, and the great things that are in store for her if she will only look to the main chance—your honour will not threaten me with the horse-pond any more, I hope ?"

" No, no, I spoke but in my anger," returned Elliot ; " and I have now be-thought me that you may be of some service, if you like."

" How ?"

" By carrying a letter for me to Patty," he replied.   " Your object in going to the Manor-house will not be suspected, and the thing can be done without anybody being the wiser.   But mind you, there must be no talking about it afterwards, or the stocks and whipping-post shall be your reward."

" Your honour may depend on my prudence."

" Or rather on your fear of the consequences," returned Elliot.   " However, meet me this evening about sun-set in the village, and I will have the letter ready for you, with further instructions that you will do well to remember."

Richard Elliot then continued his way, not altogether sorry for a meeting that he had at first been disposed to avoid. His mind was now full of Patty, whose charms had made a deep impression upon his heart ; but he was a libertine in principle, and under the assurance of an honourable passion, he was seeking to add a too confiding girl to the list of those who had already become the victims of his treacherous professions.

It was near breakfast time when Florence Campbell returned to the Clockhouse—for so was the residence of her father designated, from the huge bell with which it was surmounted—and having thrown aside the cloak and bonnet in which she had disguised herself for the interview with her lover, she entered the parlour in which her sister Laura was anxiously waiting her presence.

"Dear Florence," she cried, "why do you take these long rambles so early in the morning? There is some mystery in all this which I would fain discover, yet even a sister is considered unworthy to be your confidant. You are more serious than it was your wont to be, and I cannot but confess that my mind is filled with apprehensions that I in vain seek to banish from it."

"Try to think the best of me, and all shall be explained to your satisfaction," answered Florence. "I may appear less gay than I used to be, but there is a reason for it; and though you regret my want of confidence, you shall never have cause to reproach me for doing aught that even a sister shall deem an act of imprudence."

"I can guess who is at the bottom of it all," exclaimed Laura, "and sorry am I that you should continue to give encouragement to one whom our father brought us hither to avoid."

"And was it not an act of cruel tyranny," cried Florence, "to sever those whose happiness depends upon their union?"

"You wrong our father by thus misjudging his motives," returned her sister. "The truth is, there is more reason than you are willing to admit for the dislike which has been formed against your lover. Has he not been devoted to the gaming-table, and do we not hear that even worse crimes have been alleged against him?"

"The world speaks indifferently of him," replied Florence; "but was he not the associate of our father, whose propensities, unfortunately, also tend to deep play, and who himself introduced him to our house, well knowing the worst that a censorious world had said of him?"

"It is but too true," sighed Laura; "yet knowing what we do of him, it became the duty of a prudent woman to guard her heart against encouraging the addresses of such a man."

"You know him not, dear Laura," cried her sister, "or you would scarcely speak thus harshly of one who merits your kindest thoughts. At all events I do not see that he is more deserving of censure than is Mr. Stephen Harland, of whom you seem to think so highly."

"I speak only of Mr. Harland as others do," answered Laura, in a tone of gentle reproach, "and you surely cannot believe that I entertain a stronger feeling than respect for a person whom we have only occasionally met when strolling out."

"I only know," answered her sister, playfully, "that when we do chance to meet, you always appear to be very much agitated, and your voice trembles as it never does at any other time."

"I will admit all that," replied the blushing girl; "but it is only because I find myself in the presence of a man, whose many excellent qualities have rendered him a sort of petted favourite with everybody."

"And a favourite he certainly is of yours, if not something more," returned Florence. "I saw him this morning walking with Mr. Beaumont, and a more love-lorn looking youth it was never my good fortune to encounter. I wonder, dear Laura, if you were the subject of his contemplation."

"Why should you think anything of the kind?"

"Really that is more than I can explain; but such was my notion on seeing him, and, for a trifle, I could have found it in my heart to put him into extacies, by telling him what you have lately said of him."

"Surely," cried Laura, "you would not bring shame on me by betraying my confidence?"

"Why no," answered her sister, "but I should like to have seen how he would look when I told him that you extolled his handsome person."

"Forbear, dear Florence!" cried the other; "and do not make me ashamed of myself for having repeated what others have said before me."

"But others do not love him as you do though," answered her sister, archly. "Nay, deny it not, for 'tis only very lately when we were speaking of his supposed poverty, you said that the excellence of his heart would be more than a recompence for any fortune that might be brought him by the woman who has the happiness to become his wife."

"Well," replied Laura, "it must be confessed I did say so, but the words were uttered without any particular meaning."

"But I suppose," continued Florence, "there is a particular meaning in your having a portrait of the young gentlemen, drawn by your own hands. More than once I have caught you taking a sly peep at it, and then, mercy on me! what a sigh you give as you look upon the handsome countenance of this Stephen Harland. So, deny it as you will, dear sister of mine, this youth is not quite so indifferent to you as you would have me believe."

"I have been a thoughtless, foolish girl, I believe," answered Laura, "but you have awakened me to my error, and I will henceforth learn to think less of one in whom I have perhaps taken too great an interest. So now let me caution you once more against encouraging the addresses of Paul Rayland, whose character and former life should be a sufficient warning of the miseries a union with him must incur. Banish him for ever from your mind, and both our father and myself will rejoice at an escape from a bad man's evil designs. I have thought Stephen Harland might some day or other ask your hand, and believe me, dear Florence, there is nothing in the world that would afford me such sincere gratification as to see you become the wife of that excellent man."

"I feel assured, dear Laura," answered her sister, "that you speak with all sincerity, but it is a more difficult task than you imagine to drive from my heart the image of this much slandered Paul Rayland."

"The reports circulated against him are, I fear, below the real standard of his crimes," replied Laura. "I have been unwilling to wound your feelings before, but it is now absolutely necessary that you should know the utter worthlessness of him who has obtained this fatal hold upon your affections. He is at this moment a fugitive, endeavouring to conceal himself from the officers of justice, who are in active pursuit of him. He is known to have been the proprietor of a low gaming-house, where the unwary have been robbed to an incredible amount by the base artifices to which he has had resource. Of his guilt there can be no doubt, and as a clue to his retreat has been obtained, there is every reason to believe that a very short time will serve to place him in the hands of justice. Yet this is the man, Florence, whom you have taken to your heart, and who, I grieve to say, was introduced to us by our father."

Irresolute what answer to make, Florence remained silent and evidently suffering under the tortures to which her heart was subjected. At length, however, observing that her sister was waiting for a reply, she said,—

"All that you have been telling me I was before aware of. Paul Rayland, when young and inexperienced in the world's way, may have erred, but he has seen the folly of his career, and all that people now say of him is false, and uttered only to ruin him in the estimation of those who have hitherto regarded him with some favour. I have reflected deeply upon the subject, Laura, and find it a harder task than you imagine to abandon him when now, more than ever, he needs the countenance and support of those whom he regards."

"You have not forgotten," said Laura, "what our father told us of what occurred during the youth of this Paul Rayland—or Paul the Reckless, as I have sometimes heard him called. He committed a forgery, was tried for it, and escaped by a mere miracle. And it must still be in your remembrance how agitated our father was when he first made the discovery that you loved each other; what a fearful scene of rage followed, and what curses he invoked upon his head if he ever dared aspire to the hand of his child."

"I remember all but too well," answered Florence, with a groan of anguish; "yet

my heart is stubborn, and in spite of every effort, I find that I cannot banish Paul from my mind."

"Nay, this is weakness," cried her sister, "and a slight effort only is required to make you all that I could wish. Perhaps you are afraid of incurring his vengeance ; but be of good heart, Florence, and remember you have a father to protect you from the anger of an enfuriated ruffian. I will myself watch over you with a sister's love, and all I ask in return is, that you will make me your confidant."

"We will speak upon this subject another time," said Florence, "when you may perhaps find me more tractable than at present. The task you would impose upon me is an exceedingly difficult one, yet it shall be seriously debated in my own mind, and I will even try to forget Paul Rayland, though my heart should break in the effort. I will not promise entire submission, dear Laura ; but, at all events, you shall see that I am not unwilling to make an attempt, though it seems to be almost a hopeless one."

With tearful eyes Florence Campbell left the room, and proceeded to her chamber, where she so far gave way to her grief as to remain a voluntary prisoner during the remainder of the day.

CHAPTER II.

What doth ensue
But moody and dull melancholy,
Kinsman to grim and comfortless despair?—*Comedy of Errors.*

QUITTING the Clock-house and its inmates for a brief period, we must now follow in the footsteps of Mr. Beaumont, and his young friend, Stephen Harland, who, it will be remembered, were seen by Florence during her stolen interview with Paul the Reckless in the haunted hollow. Mr. Beaumont was a man who, from disappointments in early life, had imbibed certain unfavourable notions of his fellow-creatures, that caused him to be shunned by most of the persons with whom he had once come in contact. It must not, however, be supposed that he had utterly fallen out with mankind, for he was a warm, faithful friend wherever he formed an attachment, and it so happened that Stephen Harland was one among the favoured few to whom the honour of his better feelings was extended. On the present occasion he had by accident met with Stephen during the early walk in which he commonly indulged, and a conversation arose between them which will explain those portions of the younger man's history that are necessary to be understood at this early period of our narrative.

"You know, my dear Stephen," resumed Mr. Beaumont, after rather a long pause, "that I am rather apt to take a one-sided view of the actions of my fellow-men, but at the same time you must admit that the opinions I occasionally express are given in all fairness, though you may sometimes think my picture a little over-coloured."

"True, sir," answered Stephen; "but your opinions of the fairer portions of the creation are ——"

"Sadly ungallant, I will confess," interrupted the old gentleman. "I see them as they really are, and you, among many others, are not inclined to place much reliance on my experience. I have often warned you against falling in love, Stephen Harland, and again I say, beware of woman's allurements as you would avoid certain destruction."

"At present," replied Stephen, laughing at the vehemence with which this was uttered, "I believe you have very little to fear in that respect. I am too poor to marry, and having my way to make in the world I must be content to remain in single blessedness till I am able to support a wife in comfort and respectability. My father's affairs were left in a very unsettled state, and when they are arranged to the satisfaction of his creditors, I shall have barely sufficient to establish me in a profession."

"That shall be my care, so say nothing more about it till the proper time arrives," exclaimed the old gentleman. "I am indebted to your father, though I dare say you know nothing at all about it. You shall have the money when I see an opportunity for you to lay it out to advantage; but, at the same time, I shall make it a condition that you do not make a fool of yourself by falling head over ears in love with the first girl you happen to meet with. But I dare say the worthy vicar, who took so much care of your education in all other matters, did not fail to teach you the danger of marriage."

"He never spoke to me upon the subject," replied Stephen; "but tell me, sir, was the vicar my father, for circumstances have occurred to throw doubts on my mind that I am now most anxious to have cleared up? It is true he was ever like a parent to me, and at his death left me whatever may remain after his affairs are honourably settled. Among other things, I have this memorandum, but whether it will ever be of any service to me, you, perhaps, may be the best able to judge."

"Humph!" ejaculated the old gentleman, glancing over the paper, "it is here set forth that Major Campbell, of the Clock-house, stands indebted to the late vicar, or rather to you, as his residuary legatee, in the sum of seven hundred pounds, advanced to him at various periods. The major is a gambler, Stephen, and, as such, is scarcely to be depended on, though I dare say he would discharge the debt if it is in his power to do so. That, however, may not be the case for some time to come, and, in the meanwhile, I will advance you part, or, if necessary, the whole of the money. Hush! let me not hear a word of refusal, for I am tolerably resolute when once I say a thing, and it will be at the hazard of offending me if you say a word against my proposition."

"Your kindness, sir, fills me with gratitude," exclaimed the young man; "but when I consider the probability that I may never be able to return the money, I feel bound to ——"

"You are going to offend me, Stephen, by a blank refusal of my offer," interrupted Mr. Beaumont; "but beware what you say, or you will lose a friend who feels a sincere interest in your welfare. Change the subject, young man, and tell me why you doubt that the vicar was your parent."

"Because he made no reply when I asked him the question on his death-bed," answered Stephen. "The subject, too, seemed to be one that occasioned him a good deal of uneasiness, and involved, as I am, in uncertainty, I am now most anxious that the truth should be revealed."

"Let that subject remain as it is," exclaimed Mr. Beaumont, "for be assured there is some weighty reason against it, or you would not have been kept so long in the dark. You have your own way to work in the world; do it honourably, and, when the proper time arrives, I have no doubt you will be fully informed upon the subject that you are so exceedingly anxious about."

"And you think," said Stephen, "that Major Campbell will pay this money?"

"I can scarcely doubt it," answered Mr. Beaumont; "for, though he is a gamester, and otherwise bears but an indifferent character, he will not bring open dishonour upon himself, by refusing to discharge a just debt. However, we will take an early opportunity of calling upon him, and we shall then hear what chance there is of success or failure. In my house you will find a home for the present, and, bye-and-bye, I will take steps for establishing you in some profession that may serve you as a stepping-stone to fame, as well as riches."

"You will find me but a poor companion," returned Stephen. "I will, however, do my best to repay the many obligations I am under to you, and never shall I forget the kindness that has been bestowed upon one who has had but few friends in the world."

There was indeed a degree of mystery connected with Stephen Harland, that none could fathom, though many were the rumours circulated respecting him. At first it was believed that he was the vicar's son, but afterwards came out the truth that the worthy clergyman had never entered the state of matrimony, and the blameless life he led silenced every thought that he might be the offspring of illicit love. It afterwards was rumoured that the child had been brought to the vicarage at a very early age, but from whence he came no one was able to offer an opinion, and in spite of every inquiry that was made upon the subject, no clue could be discovered by which the mystery might be cleared up. The education bestowed on the youth by the vicar, was such a one as might fit him for the higher walks of life, and, the boy's natural talents being excellent, he made rapid progress.

Whilst yet a boy, he formed a friendship for Edward Cavendish, a youth of nearly his own age, and as their intimacy ripened, and grew stronger with each succeeding day, they began to regard each other as brothers, and could scarcely endure a separation even for a single day. They even became fellow collegians, studied together, and together obtained the honours due to their diligence and perseverance. At length they finished their college career; shortly after which, the vicar died, and Stephen Harland became, as we have seen, an inmate beneath the hospitable roof of Mr. Beaumont, whose singular manners had made him the wonder of the whole neighbourhood.

But though people regarded him with amazement, all acknowledged that in charitable acts he was ever foremost among the benevolent. That he was rich, too, no one could doubt, for a great deal of the land thereabout was owned by him. One thing could not fail to excite observation, he seemed to have neither friends nor relations, or, if he had, they never came to visit him in the secluded place he had chosen for his residence.

Among those who were most anxious to learn some of the particulars respecting him was his housekeeper, who, to do her justice, lost no opportunity to make a discovery, however trifling it might be. But there was one thing which came under her own knowledge, and this she would sometimes relate to her very particular friends, as a secret that was on no account to be divulged to any other person. It seemed from her own narrative that she had been housekeeper to Mr. Beaumont somewhere about four-and-twenty years, and shortly after taking those duties upon herself, her master absented himself from home for some days, and at length returned in a carriage accompanied by a sick lady, who was evidently in the last stage of mortal suffering. He seemed to be deeply affected at the sad situation to which she was reduced, spoke tenderly to her, was a constant watcher by her bed-side, till death terminated her existence. She was then buried in the church-yard of the parish in which she died, and where a handsome monument was erected to her memory by Mr. Beaumont. Thither it was his almost daily habit to direct his steps, and deeply did he seem to deplore the loss of her whose mysterious arrival had afforded fresh food for the wonder of those who could not even imagine a cause for the excessive grief he manifested at the loss of an apparent stranger.

Patty, of whom mention has already been made, became a domestic in the establishment of this eccentric being, and it was shortly afterwards that she became acquainted with Richard Elliot, whose motives for paying her such marked attentions were none of the most honourable. Their meetings had been held secretly, but they did not long escape the lynx-eyed vigilance of the old gentleman, who now kept a more vigilant watch upon the actions of the libertine, in order to assure himself of the designs entertained by the heartless gallant. He only wished to be thoroughly convinced that his suspicions were well founded, and in that case Mr. Richard Elliot might prepare himself for such a castigation as his perfidious conduct justly merited.

CHAPTER III.

Here is a father now,
Will truck his daughter for a foreign venture,
Make her the stop-gap to some cankered feud,
Or fling her o'er, like Jonah, to the fishes,
To appease the sea at highest.—ANON.

IT was in the evening of the same day on which occurred the conversation between the two sisters, narrated at the latter part of the first chapter, that Major Campbell returned in a state of agitation, that proved something had occurred more than ordinary. Entering the library, he paced up and down with rapid and uneven footsteps, muttering fierce invectives, and pressing his burning forehead as if the thoughts that rushed through his brain were too terrible for endurance.

"Curses on my evil fortune!" he at length exclaimed; "the ruin I have so long tried to stem off now threatens to overwhelm and crush me. All is lost with the last throw of the dice, and ruin stares me in the face, unless Laura will step forward to relieve me from the fearful penalty of my infatuation. This Lord Danebury has ever had the luck to win from me, and now honour demands that I reduce myself to beggary, unless any means can be devised as a peace-offering between us. The old dotard loves my daughter Laura, and would wed her if she can be prevailed upon to unite herself with one whom she can never regard except with coldness and disdain. Yet it must be so—she shall wed him, or the eternal maledictions of her beggared father will rest upon her head. She, too, has money over which I have no control, yet must she advance me the few thousands I want to pay my debts to his lordship, and enable me to try once more if fortune has indeed abandoned me."

As he concluded this train of wild thought, Laura entered the room, and welcomed his return home with all the affectionate ardour of a fond child.

" Father," she exclaimed, as her eye encountered his wild and haggard countenance, " you are ill, very ill—say, what has occurred to bring about this sad change in the brief period of your absence ?"

" Nothing," he replied, hoarsely; " I am well, my girl, though somewhat fatigued from the effects of a hard ride home. Nay, I assure you I am happy, though perhaps I might have been more so had your sister come to welcome my return as well as yourself."

" Florence is not aware that you are at home," answered Laura, " or she would have been here before me. She has been ill to-day, and I prevailed upon her to go early to bed, scarcely knowing whether we should see you till to-morrow."

" Are you sure of what you say ?" demanded her father; " or has she gone to meet some new lover, whose villany is even deeper than the one I have already forbidden to enter my doors ?"

" I saw her but now in bed," answered Laura, " and would have roused her to let her know that you had returned, but she looked pale as the very pillow that supports her head, and I could not find it in my heart to wake her, even though I feared you would be angry at what may appear to be her indifference to your return home. But to-morrow I hope she will be better, and you will then see how gladly she will greet your presence."

" To-morrow will be too late," he gloomily replied, " for with the earliest dawn of day I must hasten back to London."

" So soon !" said Laura; " can you then have business so urgent that you must eave us almost as soon as you return ? But I see you are agitated. What is it, dear father ? Tell me the cause, and I may perhaps have it in my power to remove it."

" I scarcely know how to utter the confession," he replied; " but it must be done, whatever you may think of me when all is told. The truth is, Laura, I have been unfortunate of late, and am involved in difficulties, from which I do not see any ready way to extricate myself unless you will nobly step forward to my rescue. You must lend me money, girl : a few hundreds will answer my present exigencies, and I shall be able to return it all in the course of a few hours. Give me an order on the person who holds your property, and when this cursed difficulty has been got over, I will make arrangements for returning what I am now obliged to borrow. So sit you down, Laura—here are pens, ink, and paper, and by scribbling a few lines you will save a father from the dishonour that he regards as ten thousand times worse than death."

" 'Tis a child's first duty to minister to a parent's wants or necessities," answered Laura, " and perhaps I may be exceeding my duty in attempting to remonstrate with him to whom I am so deeply indebted. Yet, oh, my dear father, pause, I beseech you, ere irretrievable ruin is brought down upon our house. I know the dreadful consequences that ever attend the life of a professed gamester,—that poverty and destruction are continually staring him in the face—that even the worst of crimes, self murder, but too freequently closes his career when all hope of retrieving himself is at an end."

" This preaching is all in vain, girl," exclaimed her father, angrily ;—" my circumstances are desperate, and something must be done to extricate me, or I become degraded and dishonoured amongst those who will not fail to report my fallen fortunes to the whole world."

" And will the assistance you have asked of me entirely relieve all your pressing necessities ?" asked the sorrowing girl.

" It will," he replied; " for when I have paid Lord Danebury the sum I lost to him, I have a scheme to put in practice that will not only put me once more upon my legs, but will also be of the greatest advantage to yourself. The nobleman to whom I have alluded, and in whose eyes I would seem to be a man of honour, is a wealthy widower, and there is good reason to believe he wants to confer a high honour upon me. In truth, my dear Laura, he wishes to form a connection with my family, and I scarcely need tell you how anxious I am to forward views that will prove so advantageous to myself."

"It was scarcely necessary to explain yourself so far to your daughter," replied Laura, "since I feel but too happy that it is in my power to do your bidding with so small a sacrifice on my own part. Here is the paper you asked for, and may it bring peace and happiness to a heart that I fear has known little joy for many a long day past."

"A thousand thanks, dear Laura," exclaimed Major Campbell, as he placed the note in his pocket-book. "And now tell me, dear child, have you formed any notion of the plan I have in view?"

"I can only guess, sir," she replied, "that you are about to form a matrimonial alliance with the family of Lord Danebury."

"Humph! You think then, of course, that I am about to marry again?"

"From what you have said," answered Laura, "I can arrive at no other conclusion."

"Well, then, you must think me a greater simpleton than I really am," he replied. "No, no, my dear girl—I have told you that his lordship is a widower, and from certain hints that he has dropped, I can entertain no doubts that he is on the point of asking your hand in marriage."

"Indeed!"

"Ah!" exclaimed her father, "I thought I should be able to give you an agreeable surprise. The honour, it must be admitted, is both great and unexpected; but why should not the young and accomplished Laura Campbell assume the coronet as well as many others I could name?"

"My dear father," she replied, with emotion, "that your zeal in forwarding this proposed match is well intended, I have every inclination to believe. I, however, feel no inclination to exalt myself to the high station you have spoken of; my disposition leads me to seek a more humble and quiet path in life, and should I ever wed—which at present seems very doubtful—it must be with one whose worth alone shall render him acceptable in my eyes."

"You speak like a foolish, inexperienced girl, as you are," exclaimed her father, with mingled anger and surprise. "The worth of which you speak is, I admit, an excellent ingredient in man's composition; but may we not find it in the peer as well as the peasant? Beware, Laura, how you excite my indignation by a blind opposition to my will! Your sister, Florence, has thought proper to disregard my commands, with respect to her rejection of Paul Rayland; she still loves him, in spite of all I have said, and the consequences will fall upon her own head."

"Oh, speak not thus harshly of the sister I so fondly love!" cried Laura;—"at all events, wait awhile, and I will do all in my power to frustrate a step that can lead to nothing but ruin and dishonour."

"It is of *you* that I would now speak," exclaimed Major Campbell; "for the marriage I have spoken of is the one thought that occupies my mind to the exclusion of everything else. The chance presented to you is one that is never likely to be offered again, and, therefore, must not be thrown away for any trifling caprice. It is your father's wish—nay, his most imperative command, that you give this subject a careful and deliberate consideration, and when you have done that, I have no doubt you will do all that a fond father desires for the advancement of your own fortune."

"Has Lord Danebury spoken to you upon the subject?" asked Laura, timidly.

"He has indirectly adverted to it," replied her father, "and the manner in which he always speaks of it, convinces me that the moment has nearly arrived when he will formally make the proposition. Indeed, that was the cause of my agitation when you first came into the room, for I trembled at the thought of not being able to discharge the debt of honour due to him, and, had I proved a defaulter, there would, of course, have been an end of the glorious project that had cost me so many anxious hours. Thanks, however, to your timely assistance, I shall now be able to fulfil my engagements to him, and then I have every reason to believe he will immediately declare his sentiments."

"And this," cried Laura, "is the only ground you have for believing that Lord Danebury has an intention to seek alliance with one whose station in life is far beneath his own ?"

"It is not the only reason I have," answered her father, "though I could have wished to have been spared a further explanation at present. However, the truth is, his lordship believes I am possessed of a very handsome fortune, which, no doubt, is the chief source of attraction. So far I have contrived to keep up the deception by mere outward show, though certainly at some inconvenience to myself. But my purpose has been served, and it will soon remain with yourself to declare whether the commands of a father are to be obeyed."

"All reasonable commands I shall ever obey most cheerfully," replied Laura ; "but in this instance I see so many objections, that I almost fear it will not be in my power to render the submission you desire."

"What objections do you see ?" demanded her father, hastily.

"By your own admission," answered Laura, "his lordship has been deceived into a belief that you are possessed of great wealth. The real situation of your affairs cannot be much longer concealed, if he makes any inquiry, and then think what shame and misery will be brought upon your child by this hated marriage of ambition."

"You are too sensitive upon a matter that scarcely requires a thought," exclaimed Major Campbell. "If the marriage takes place, my object will be accomplished, and it will puzzle all the lawyers in England to deprive Lady Danebury of her title, whilst her own character as a virtuous wife remains untainted. So reflect well upon what I have said, and when next we see each other, let me hear from your own lips that my commands are to be obeyed."

"I will make no promise," said Laura ; "but you may be assured I will give the subject my most careful consideration."

And thus ended an interview in which a father threw aside the mask he had assumed, and openly avowed himself a cool, calculating villain.

CHAPTER IX.

This, by his tongue, should be a Montague!
Fetch me my rapier, boy ;
Now, by the faith and honour of my kin,
To strike him dead I hold it not a sin.—*Romeo and Juliet.*

AT the usual hour on the following morning, Mr. Beaumont left his bed, and having dressed himself, he knocked at Stephen's door with a tremendous clatter, and desiring him to follow in the direction of the village church, he left the Manor House, and had just passed through the garden-gate, when he saw an aged female lurking about the premises, under rather suspicious circumstances. He at once recognized her as the old gipsy who has before been introduced to the notice of the reader, and believing that she was there for no good purpose, he strode towards the place where she was endeavouring to conceal herself, and in no very gentle tones desired her to leave the place, under a penalty of paying a visit to the parish round-house.

"Heaven save your honour," exclaimed the old woman ; "what have I done to deserve this rough treatment ?"

"It's not what you have done, but what you are going to do," answered Mr. Beaumont. "Like myself, you are an early riser, it seems ; but your object in coming here is mischief, so tramp away as fast as your legs will carry you, or it's likely there will be leisure to repent that you have come here on your infernal errand of mischief."

"I wouldn't harm your honour for the world," exclaimed the gipsy; "and the only reason that you find me here is to tell the fortune of some of your servants, who would like to know what's going to happen to them."

"Can you tell what's going to happen to yourself?" demanded the old gentleman, impatiently.

"No harm, I hope."

"Harm!" he exclaimed; "you are a pretty hussy, truly, to profess that you can tell the fortunes of other people, and yet not know your own."

"We are not allowed to know our own destiny," replied the gipsy; "but the stars guide those that are initiated in the mysteries of science, and there are other signs that we who belong to the craft can clearly understand."

"I can clearly understand that you are an old impostor," exclaimed Mr. Beaumont; "and why I stand here talking instead of sending you before a magistrate, is more than I can make out. So troop, thou hag of darkness, troop, I say, and save yourself, before I call to those who will make a clearance in spite of your charms and nonsense."

"Your people dread my power," replied the woman, "and there's not one among them would lay hands upon me, for fear of what might follow. I could give them aching bones that should last long enough to make them sorry for laying their cursed grip upon a poor creature that is only trying to gain a crust by following her craft."

"Your craft will not save you from my displeasure if you don't hobble away beyond the reach of my arm," he said, flourishing a stout cudgel that was the usual companion of his walks. "I have no great fancy for any of your tribe, so away with you, and never let me catch you hunting after my servants again."

"Humph!" she muttered; "but there's other servants in the neighbourhood, I suppose, that I may go round among without asking your leave?"

"Ay, ay, there are plenty of fools that place faith in your lies, no doubt," he replied; "but I suppose you don't carry love letters to all of them."

"Love letters!" stammered the woman.

"Yes, love letters, thou imp of Satan!" he exclaimed, and darting forward he seized her arms, and took from her the letter which she had been commissioned by Richard Elliot to smuggle into the hands of the simple, unsuspecting Patty. "Now," he continued, "what do you think of this? Have I not read the stars as well as yourself, to discover what sort of errand it was that brought you here?"

"I felt sure beforehand," she said, "that some mischief would come of all this. But I'm a fool for my pains, and as your honour has found me out, I'll make the best of my way from this place, lest I should meet the sender of the letter, who would half strangle me if I was to tell him that I had not wit enough to do his errand cleverly."

"Ha! ha!" exclaimed the old gentleman, as he finished reading the love epistle; "so Mr. Richard Elliot is the *gentleman* that comes hunting about the house for my servants. I suspected him before, but now that I have found him out, he had better keep at a respectable distance, or he may have cause to be sorry that he ever set eyes upon that poor senseless woman-creature, Patty."

"Surely your honour wouldn't go fighting at your time of life?"

"No, no; I should not raise my arm against him, that I know of," answered Mr. Beaumont; "but that would depend upon himself, for I have a peppery spirit of my own, and if he should provoke me there's no saying what passion would drive me to."

"But, saving your honour's presence ——"

"Out upon you, hag! why do you stay here when I have so often warned you to begone?"

"I was only going to say," replied the gipsy, "that as I've not given the letter as I promised, the gentleman will refuse to pay me the reward."

"And serve you right, too," answered Mr. Beaumont. "However, here's half-a-crown for you since the mischief you came for has been defeated, and remember, from this time forward I shall keep a sharp look out round the premises, and if you, or any of your gang, should be found lurking about, I'll see that the parish stocks don't lie idle much longer. You understand me, old woman, and, recollect, when once I say a thing I always keep to it."

"Bless your reverence," exclaimed the woman, "I have no wish to come if you have any objection to your maids having their fortune told; the world is wide enough for us all, so a fair good morning to you, and if any of your silver spoons should be stolen, you have only to send for me, and maybe I may be able to tell you something about 'em."

"That's about the most likely thing of anything you have said," muttered Mr. Beaumont, as he resumed his walk towards the church. His thoughts then recurred to Patty and the villain who was seeking her ruin, when advancing footsteps awakened him from the reflection, and, looking up, who should be standing a few paces before him, but Mr. Richard Elliot himself.

"We are well met," exclaimed the libertine, who was ever ready with a falsehood whenever it would serve his purpose. "I was just going down to your house to ask your advice upon a subject that I've been a good deal perplexed about."

"Indeed!" retorted the other, with a sneer; "some little love adventure, I'll dare be sworn."

"Nay," laughed Elliot, "love is the very last subject upon which I would consult a man who I believe has not the highest opinion of the fair sex."

"There you are mistaken, sir," returned Mr. Beaumont, "for I entertain a high respect for them, though I could wish so many were not spoiled by the adulation of fellows upon two legs that have the presumption to call themselves men. But, go on, sir, you were about to tell me the business that was taking you to my house."

"I have been offered a small freehold adjoining some property of yours," replied Elliot, "and I would merely inquire whether you have any particular wish to purchase it, as in that case I should decline the offer, and ——"

"Stop, sir, if you please, and let me hear no more lies where there is no necessity for them."

"Lies!" exclaimed the other, his eyes flashing with resentment; "beware, sir, how you insult one who has both the power and the inclination to chastise such impertinence."

"I doubt neither your power nor inclination to commit an act of violence upon a man old enough to be your grandfather," replied Mr. Beaumont. "I have certainly charged you with telling a falsehood, because I happen to know there is not an acre of land to be sold anywhere in the neighbourhood. But I know your errand to my house, and if you doubt my word, here is your letter to Patty that I just now took from the old woman that was bribed to be your messenger of love."

Mr. Richard Elliot was what is vulgarly called "flabbergasted," as his own veritable handwriting was held up to view, and it was not without some little difficulty that he could retain sufficient command over himself to make a reply. At length, however, after a good deal of stuttering and stammering, he said,—

"Ah, ah—yes—I see—that letter is certainly mine—but—a—a—it was only meant by way of a little innocent joke."

"Indeed!" quoth Mr. Beaumont; "but it strikes me the joke might have been a very serious one if it had not been for this fortunate discovery. So, in future, Mr. Richard Elliot, I will be obliged to you to keep these little innocent jests, as you call them, out of my establishment, or this sort of business may turn out less droll than you seem to think it at present."

"Why, you ain't serious, are you, old crusty?"

"That will be seen, if you don't take my advice in good time," replied Mr. Beaumont. "You bear the character, sir, of being a keen sportsman, but beware how you come poaching upon any part of my property, for I have an utter aversion for such characters as you, and may, perhaps, give further proof of it, if we should happen to meet again under circumstances similar to the present."

"But you won't allow me to explain myself."

"I want no explanation, sir," replied the old gentleman, "because I should only have to listen to a parcel of falsehoods that would put me more out of temper than I am. Let it suffice that I know you, Mister Richard Elliot, and it is not all your flummery and fine words that will ever convince me you are an honest man."

"You are welcome to think just as you please of me," returned the other, with cool insolence, "for as it was never my ambition to obtain the favour of Mr. Beaumont, I can have no desire to worm myself into his good graces. It may, however, be as well to caution you against raising any reports to my prejudice, as I shall know how to resent an injury done to my character."

"Character!"

"Ay, sir—I have one, I suppose?"

"Yes, Mr. Elliot, and a d—d bad one too, I can tell you," returned the old gentleman. "Not that I should have taken the trouble to say anything about it, if it had not been for your own foolish vapouring and vaunting. But I suppose we now perfectly understand each other, and as your love epistle has not reached its destination, it would be useless to go in search of Patty, who was sent off last night to a distant farm-house, and may not return for some hours. So, your way home, sir, lies over yonder fields, and when I have seen you fairly out of harm's way, I shall resume my walk, which this meeting has somewhat interrupted."

Growling out a hearty curse or two, Richard Elliot turned away, and took the direction that led towards the Haunted Hollow, where he thought it possible he might meet with Patty on her return home, if, indeed, she had been sent away as the old gentleman had said. Mr. Beaumont continued to watch him till he was fairly out of sight, and being by that time joined by Stephen Harland, they pursued their way towards the church.

"How far do you intend to walk, sir, this morning?" asked Stephen, by way of breaking a silence that began to grow tedious.

"The Clock-house is my intended destination," replied the other.

"The Clock-house!" exclaimed Stephen, with surprise. "Does Major Campbell expect to see us?"

"Not unless he possesses the power of foretelling events," replied the old gentleman. "It is not a visit of form that I am going to pay, but one of business, and as the major frequently leaves home for London at an early hour in the morning, I thought it would be better to catch him without giving any intimation of our intended call."

Here the conversation dropped, and in a few minutes afterwards Mr. Beaumont and his young friend arrived at the Clock-house, when the former, at his own request, was conducted to the presence of Major Campbell, and the latter, to his inexpressible joy, was ushered into the breakfast-parlour, where the two young ladies were waiting the arrival of their father. As Stephen entered the room the countenance of Laura changed alternately from red to white, and in spite of all her efforts to recover herself the agitation that convulsed her frame must have been observed but for the interposition of Florence, who, with her usual gaiety, welcomed the visitor to her father's house, and accounted for her sister's trepidation by saying that she was extremely ill.

In a short time, however, Laura recovered herself sufficiently to join in the conversation, and as her confidence and animation increased Stephen began to discover perfections that till the present period he had not given her credit for. But just as they began to grow upon more familiar terms, they were interrupted by the entrance of Major Campbell and Mr. Beaumont into the room. The latter refused a pressing invitation to stop to breakfast, and bidding good morning to the host and his daughters, the old gentleman and Stephen set out on their return home. Mr. Beaumont remained for some time silent and thoughtful, but at last remembering that he had a companion with him, he said,—

"Well, Stephen, I suppose you are wondering what could have induced me to pay this early visit to Major Campbell; but you cannot have forgotten that you hold his acknowledgment for a large sum of money that he was indebted to your friend or father, the late worthy vicar, and so I thought it best that we should lose no time about it, and thus came about the stroll we have taken this morning."

"Did you speak to him upon the subject?" asked the young man.

"Oh, yes," replied Mr. Beaumont; "I went there for that purpose, and of course would not come away without performing my errand."

"Does he dispute the debt?"

"No."

"Does he acknowledge it?"

"Why, he can't do otherwise," replied the old gentleman, "since we have got his own black and white as evidence against him. I do not think, however, he much likes the claim being made upon him, for it is pretty evident that he had made up his mind that he would never be asked to return the money."

"Perhaps he is not rich enough to pay it at so short a notice," observed Stephen.

"Why, I believe money matters don't go very well with him just at present," answered Mr. Beaumont; "for, like all your professed gamesters, he is up in the stirrups one week and sprawling in the road the next. This same fortune is a mettlesome steed to ride, and not unfrequently throws us from the saddle at the very moment when we think ourselves most firmly seated."

"You think Major Campbell is in that predicament, then, I suppose ?"

" I do ; but it is possible I may be mistaken, through I could almost wager my life that he would prove insolvent if his creditors were to be too pressing for payment."

" In that case I will not urge him for the seven hundred pounds."

"Psha!" exclaimed Mr. Beaumont, "you are a foolish inexperienced boy, and know no more of business than you did the first day you were born ! Suppose you were to forgive him the seven hundred pounds he owes, it would be just so much more to throw away, as he has done with all the rest of his money, and would not keep him from ruin a single hour. These gamblers, Stephen, are desperate fellows, and the more fortune frowns upon them the more enamoured do they seem to grow of her, and, as a final resource, they throw their last few hundreds into the scale, and if it is not sufficient to kick the beam, they rise from the table ruined men ; some of them seeking death by their own hands, and others finding an asylum in Bedlam, where they linger out a miserable existence, unpitied by all who loathe the dreadful infatuation."

"But, in the event of the major's ruin, what is to become of his daughters ?" asked Stephen.

"Why, I believe both the girls have got a small fortune, independent of their father," answered the old gentleman. "Besides, they will get husbands to take care of them, no doubt. I have not yet heard whether Laura has any fellow dangling after her, but Florence, it seems, has made a pretty choice, and is too self-willed to see her error. She has fallen in love with that scoundrel, Paul Rayland ; but if he hasn't the devil's luck and his own too, he will be in our county gaol before he is many hours older."

"Is a pursuit made after him ?" inquired Stephen Harland.

"Ay, and an active one," answered Mr. Beaumont ; "and if they catch him he'll meet with no quarter, for he has long been carrying on a swindling game ; and the charge now against him is for cheating Edward Cavendish, your friend, out of a few hundreds. It seems Paul met with the young man in London, and prevailed on him to accompany him to a gaming-house that it turns out belonged to himself, and where he has for some time past carried on a complete system of robbery. He is now a fugitive from justice, yet I hope a very little time longer will serve to make him fast enough in prison. But here we are at home, Stephen, so we must break off our conversation, and you shall hear the rest over the breakfast table."

———

CHAPTER V.

He skulks, sir, near at hand,
For hereabouts he entered, and the place
Affords fair scope for hiding from our search.—*Don Raymond.*

UPON parting from Florence Campbell on the morning of their interview in the Haunted Hollow, Paul Rayland dived into the thickest part of the copse lest he should chance to meet with any of the persons who were in pursuit of him. Even the shaking of a bough filled him with apprehension, and so assured did he feel that his danger was greater than he had at first expected, that at length escaping into a dry ditch that was thickly overgrown with bushes, he determined to remain there until some of his companions should pass ; or, if no friend came in search of him, to lie in his place of concealment till the darkness of night should serve to shield him from the search that was being made for him by the officers of justice.

But in spite of his determination the time passed away heavily enough in his uncomfortable hiding-place, and after three or four hours had slowly passed away he was thinking of venturing out of his lurking-place in order to relieve his cramped limbs, when some one was heard approaching, and as he crept still closer to avoid discovery, a low whistle near at hand announced the presence of a companion that he had long been expecting.

"All's right, Paul," exclaimed the man; "so, wherever you are hiding yourself, jump out, and let an old comrade see that you are safe and sound."

"I am safe enough at present," said Paul, creeping from his hiding-place; "but, to tell you the truth, most confoundedly tired of doubling myself up in this confounded ditch. I expected you long enough ago with news as to how the land lies."

"But I couldn't get here sooner," replied Rough Rob, "for the traps are sneaking about after you, and if I hadn't taken care you'd have found yourself in the wrong box, I can tell you; and that would have been a good deal worse than lying comfortable and snug in a good dry ditch where nobody would ever think of looking after you."

"Which way are they searching after me?" asked Paul, after he had looked cautiously round to satisfy himself that no one besides themselves was near.

"Oh, in every direction," answered Rob; "they know they've got a shy bird to look after, so there's plenty engaged in the job, and some have been sent to one place, and some to another, to prevent giving you anything in the shape of a chance to get away. If you leave this place I wouldn't give a farthing for your life, for they'll have you, even though it be to take your dead body before the magistrates as a proof that they earned the reward that has been offered."

"And you, I dare say," returned Paul Rayland, "would hardly put forth your hand in case they should happen to pounce upon me unawares."

"I should do my best to do you a service," replied the other; "but if once the chaps could find out your hiding-place it would soon be all over. It seems they owe you a long score, and will not forget to pay it if you only give 'em the opportunity. There's that little matter of the forgery to answer for, and you'd have been hanged at the time if I hadn't contrived to get you into a snug place where nobody ever thought of looking after you. Ah, Paul! those were happy days, for we used to laugh and sing like merry fellows, as we were; and, at last, when the affair had blowed over, and you could venture from your hiding-place, didn't you—under another name—set up a gaming-house; and wasn't I your factotum till a certain something else happened that sent us flying again as if the devil was at our heels?"

Before Paul could make any further reply, the loud report of a pistol was heard, and a bullet passing close to them, crashed through the branches of a tree that grew close behind where they were standing. In an instant the fugitive perceived that his enemies were close at hand, and without uttering a word to his companion he plunged into the dry ditch that had before served him as a place of shelter, and scarcely had he disappeared than a couple of police officers came running forward, the foremost of whom, in an imperative tone, demanded of Rough Rob what had become of his companion.

"Companion!" reiterated the gipsy; "I don't know what your honour means by a companion."

"There was a man with you when we fired," answered the officer, "and if you don't tell us where he is, you shall go with us, and then we shall see if we can't rub up your memory a bit."

"Why, it ain't to be denied there was a man talking to me," returned Rob; "but I didn't know there was any law against people speaking when they happen to meet together."

"He is the criminal we are in pursuit of," exclaimed the officer, "and shall not escape by any of your juggling tricks. Say where he is, or you shall go to prison as one of his confederates."

"I know nothing about where he is," replied Rob; "you frightened him, I suppose, when that bullet passed so close to him, for he took to his heels as fast as he could run, and, as I think, entered yonder thicket, where I dare say you may find him if you'll only take the trouble to look well about."

"This fellow only wants to get us away that his comrade may escape in our absence," said the other officer. "I'll be bound he is lurking somewhere about this ditch, so let us both fire into it, for we must have him whether he is dead or alive."

"No, you won't, though," exclaimed the gipsy, holding up his ponderous club, threateningly; "I have had as great odds as this to fight against before now, and if either of you discharge your pistols it will be at the expense of a broken crown."

"It's clear," said the man who had first spoken, "that Paul Rayland is concealed there, and we will drive him out in spite of this fellow's threats."

"Stop for one moment," exclaimed Rob, "and don't be running the risk of killing people that have never done harm to any one. A great many of our tribe are wandering about the place,—women and children are among them, and if any harm should befal our wives or families you needn't expect to leave this place alive. You see this whistle? One shrill blast upon it will be heard from end to end of the hollow, and we shall then see which side has most cause for boasting."

"Never mind what he says," muttered one of the officers. "Paul Rayland is there, and we'll have him, let what will come of it. Hah! I see the bushes move. Fire, Dick, in that direction, and dead or alive, the fellow will be ours."

But before this threat could be put into execution, the thickly entangled branches opened, and the old gipsy woman, whom we have before introduced, crept forth, and stood erect and undaunted before them.

"Would you slay a poor old creature like me?" she exclaimed. "Shame on ye both for cowards, that would spill the blood of an aged female, that is a wanderer in this wild place only because in the wide world she has no better habitation. But 'tis well for yourselves that you didn't fire, or both of you would have come to the gallows a little sooner than you otherwise would."

"Stop your croaking, old hag, or it will be the worse for you," growled one of the officers. "We are here in search of a criminal, and all those that aid in preventing his capture are subject to a long imprisonment for their pains."

"It would be dangerous to lay hands on me, though," replied the old woman; "for there's plenty hereabouts that would prevent my falling into your hands."

"You're a fool for holding parley with 'em," exclaimed Rob, with a scowl that was meant to awe her. "These people are foes to our race, so go your ways, and leave me to manage 'em after my own fashion. Hence, I say, or there'll be mischief through your interfering with things that don't concern you."

"I'll go at your bidding," answered the woman; "but it's not because I'm afraid of anything you can do. I've braved the anger of many a bolder braggart than you, before now, and would show you how little I care for your anger, if it wasn't that Paul Rayland might happen to fare all the worse for our quarrel."

Muttering to herself, the old gipsy moved away; and the officer who had first spoken to Rob asked him if he would afford a clue to the fugitive, on condition that he received a portion of the reward that had been offered for his apprehension.

"I've told you before that I know nothing at all of him," replied Rob; "so it's useless to ask me any more questions about it."

"Nonsense," replied the other; "you could tell me if you like, but the truth is, you are old cronies together, and you don't like to split upon him."

"I can't say I like treachery among comrades," answered the gipsy; "and, to tell you the truth, if I knew exactly where he is, and twenty pieces of gold were put into my hand to betray him, I should refuse the money, rather than deliver up a poor devil to the tender mercies of the law."

"Well," exclaimed the officer, "I can't say but what you are a good fellow of the sort; but we are sure to lay hold of this Paul Rayland before we give up looking for him, and so I don't see what great harm there can be in your just giving a hint that may save us some little trouble. Lead us to the place where he's lying concealed, and you shall leave us a richer man than you have ever been before."

It now struck Rob that he had an excellent opportunity to make something out of the affair, without doing an injury to his friend, and, after seeming to reflect a little upon the offer, he said,—

" How much, now, might a man expect to receive for his trouble, supposing he was to undertake the task of being your guide ?"

" Twenty pounds," replied the other.

" And when would he receive it ?"

" Directly after Paul Rayland is secured."

" Humph ! then that won't suit me," answered the gipsy, "for I've too often seen tricks played with a poor devil when he has done all he could, and if I'm to help you in this affair, I must have the money first, or there's an end of the bargain."

" We have not so much money between us," replied the officer; " but I'll tell you what bargain we'll make,—you shall have half the money now, and the remainder as soon as Paul is safely lodged in gaol."

" Agreed," exclaimed Rob, holding out his hand for the promised moiety of the reward, and laughing gleefully ; as the money was counted and given him, he added,—

" This is the best argument that I know of to convince a man against his will ; and so now, gentlemen, I am at your service."

Upon this he motioned for them to follow him ; and, placing his finger upon his lips, cautioned them not to speak, lest the fugitive should chance to hear their approach and flee to some other place, where it would not be very easy to find him.

As they moved away, Paul Rayland slowly, and without noise, raised himself sufficiently high in his lurking place to observe the direction taken by Rough Rob. He had overheard all the conversation that passed between him and the officers of justice, and it was not without certain misgivings that he watched the movements of his comrade, after he had accepted the money which had been offered for the avowed purpose of betraying him into the hands of his pursuers.

In this uncertainty, his impulse was to creep stealthily away, and seek some other refuge ; but the probability of being discovered checked the determination almost as soon as it was formed, and, upon re-consideration, he resolved to remain where he was till the return of his comrade, and then, if there should be need for it, to lose his life in a last desperate effort to escape from his pursuers. For nearly half an hour was he a prey to these uneasy reflections, when at last the well-known signal of Rough Rob was heard, and, springing from his lair, ready for any extremity, he stood face to face with the man upon whose fidelity his very existence depended.

" How now !" he exclaimed ; " am I to look upon you as a friend, or an enemy ?"

" Why a friend, to be sure," answered Rob ; " what reason have you fo thinking me a foe ?"

" Reason enough for suspecting you, at any rate," replied Paul. " You took the bribe that was offered for betraying me, and I scarcely know whether you went to point out my hiding-place, or to play some trick upon the fellows that are so hot in their pursuit of me."

" You ought to know me better than to suppose I would turn a traitor, Paul Rayland," answered the other. " No, no, I saw how things were going, and as a little money was to be made by bamboozling these officers, I thought it would not be a bad joke to pocket their offer, and then lead 'em a bit of a dance, that should end in disappointment. The poor fellows got rather tired at last, but I managed them pretty well, and to make short of a long story, you are safe for some little time, at any rate."

" Didn't they suspect you after it became evident that I was not to be found quite so easily as they expected ?"

" Why, it must be confessed they got rather impatient at last," replied Rob ;

"but I told 'em such a plausible story, that they could hardly think I was deceiving 'em."

"And how," asked Paul Rayland, "did you contrive to slip away from them at last?"

"Oh, easily enough," replied the other; "I took from 'em the power of doing me any mischief, and then laughed at 'em for their pains."

"How did you do that?"

"Why, I led the simpletons to a place where I persuaded them you were lying concealed. They believed every word I said, and then, pretending that I could see the bushes move, I advised them to fire their pistols right into the place. They did so, and then, as there was nothing to fear from their weapons, I wished them a very good day, plunged into the thickest part of the wood, and hurried here to let you know what I've been doing."

"And they will return to this place with a tolerable certainty that you have lured them away from the object of their pursuit."

"Then we must be prepared to give them a warm reception," answered Rob; "we are equal in numbers, and it will be a strange thing if we can't give 'em a taste of our mettle when we know what would be the end of it if they should happen to get the best of the fray."

"May I depend upon your standing by me to the last?" inquired Paul, with great earnestness.

"Why, to be sure you may," replied the other; "I'm just now in the humour for a bit of devilry, and nothing would please me better than to have a brush with these fellows by way of teaching them not to interfere with other people in future. But I'm inclined to think there'll be no occasion to come to close quarters just yet, for I can hear them shouting to each other some distance off, so I suppose they've managed to part company, and are making the best of their way out of the Haunted Hollow, lest they should happen to fall into an ambush."

"Then we will stay where we are for the present," answered Paul Rayland, "and prepare ourselves in case they should return with additional numbers. I have a brace of pistols here that may prove of some service in the hour of need, and being driven to desperation, I shall not fail to use them, should we be urged to choose between liberty and death."

"Ay, that's speaking out boldly, like a man," exclaimed Rob, "and I think you know enough of me to be satisfied that there'll be no want of help, should we chance to come to a scrimmage. We have fought side by side together before now, and the last time we did so must be too fresh in your memory to need repeating."

"You mean," exclaimed Paul, "the conflict we had with young Edward Cavendish, when he found out the sort of company he was keeping?"

"Yes," replied the other, "for that was a night that I rather think that none of us are likely to forget. How his eyes flashed fire when he discovered that he had been lured into our obscure gaming-house, only to be fleeced out of every farthing of money that he possessed."

"True," replied Paul; "and what a determined attitude he assumed when he saw that there was an intention on our part to keep him there as a prisoner till we could force him to take an oath never to divulge a secret that must terminate in our own utter destruction."

"And then with what desperation he fought single-handed against us, when he had made up his mind to escape from the house!" added Rough Rob. "I have had many a hard tussle in my time, but never met with such a customer as this Mr. Edward Cavendish turned out to be. At one time he had got me by the throat with so firm a grip, that I gave myself up for a dead man—and so I should have been, too, if it had not been for your assistance, when he was forced to let go his hold, and taking advantage of the opportunity, he bounded down stairs, dashed open the outer door, and rushed through the streets as if a legion of fiends had been at his heels! Hang the fellow! what trouble he gave us, and yet, after all, to escape as he did, to raise an alarm that made our old quarters too warm to hold us. However, we may be safe here for awhile, if we only act with a little caution."

"You have nothing to fear," returned Paul, "for he did not recognise you; and under your present disguise, he is not very likely to do so."

"There's where I certainly have an advantage," replied Rob, "and I only wish you had the same good fortune. But he called you by name at the moment of escape, and yet, though he lives somewhere in the neighbourhood, you have chosen this place, of all others, to hide yourself from the infernal harpies of the law."

"That," answered the fugitive, "is, because near this spot resides the maiden whom I have resolved to make mine."

"Psha!" muttered the other; "is the girl a fool that she would give her hand to a man that has been denounced as a villain?"

"Florence Campbell loves me," answered Paul, "and will share my fortunes, desperate as at present they seem to be. It is true she knows not half the crimes

I have committed, or perhaps she would begin to regard me with a different feeling. But we are running a risk here that may lead us into fresh trouble; so come and share my hiding-place till the heat of this pursuit is over, and when it is safe to leave it, I will prevail upon Florence to become the partner of my flight, when some other country may afford us a home that is denied us in England."

Rob made no further reply, and following his companion, they together crept into the hiding-place which had before sheltered the fugitive, Paul Rayland.

CHAPTER VI.

What means this insolence?
Why am I watched and dogged from place to place,
As if I were suspected of some crime
For which I had to answer?—ANONYMOUS.

IT was two days after the occurrences described in the last chapter, that Stephen Harland left the Manor-house, to visit the family of Major Campbell. Laura, as it may be imagined, was the chief source of attraction to him, for his heart had yielded to the sovereignty of her charms, and sleeping or waking, his thoughts were ever directed towards the beauteous girl who had gained this powerful ascendancy in his heart.

But these feelings, which had been newly awakened in him, he was forced to keep secret from his friend Mr. Beaumont, with whose opinion respecting love the reader has already been made acquainted. Fearful of exciting the displeasure of the old gentleman, he uttered not one word that might give rise to the least suspicion of whither he was going; and when he set out on his intended walk to the mansion of Major Campbell, he took a circuitous route that led towards the Haunted Hollow, and where the road was skirted on one side by the ancient trees that bordered on the much-dreaded spot.

Fully occupied with his thoughts, Stephen Harland passed unheedingly onward, attracted, as it were, by the fair image of Laura Campbell. At one moment his spirits were elevated at the apparent certainty of the rich reward that awaited him; but in turn these happy dreams were chased away from his mind by the probability that her love might already have been bestowed upon another. He was thus bewildering himself with a thousand perplexing notions, when he was suddenly startled at hearing his name pronounced in a loud, imperative tone, and looking up he saw a stranger issuing from a thicket a little in advance, and who, as he sprang into the road, demanded whither he was going.

"I must first know," replied Stephen, with a glance of scorn, "who it is that questions my motives, and by what right he has assumed an authority that I shall not acknowledge."

"You have heard me, Stephen Harland," exclaimed the other, "and I must have an answer before you proceed further on your way. Who I am may be explained hereafter, but who you are is a riddle that may never be solved. Let it suffice that I guess your motive for coming this road, and if you take my advice, you will turn your steps homeward, or a quarrel will ensue, in which you may happen to come off only second best."

"Leave me a clear path, fellow!" exclaimed Stephen, fiercely; "stand on one side, I say, and let me pass freely on my way, for, as there is a Heaven above us, I will not be bullied from my purpose by a ruffian who, for anything I know, may be here to rob me."

"You have nothing to fear from me in that respect," answered Paul Rayland, for it was indeed he. "I may be your friend or your foe, as circumstances shall decide; but again, I say, turn back, lest evil should come of this meeting."

"There is no evil," replied Stephen Harland, "that I am not prepared to avert. My journey this road is with a purpose, and ——"

"I know your purpose," exclaimed the other, "and am determined to oppose it. You would be my rival in love, but beware how you excite the rage of a desperate man who is resolved to accomplish his ends, even though it should be at the expense of blood."

" Your words are those of a madman," cried Stephen ; " you accuse me of being a rival, and yet, as Heaven is my witness, I have no thought of intruding upon any one with whom you may be acquainted."

" Are you not on your way to the Clock-house ?"

" I am."

" And do you deny that your visit is intended for one of the daughters of Major Campbell ?"

" It may be that you are not very far out in your guess."

" Which of the girls is it that has made so deep an impression on your heart ?"

" Humph !" retorted Stephen ; " you must produce some better authority before I answer any more of these insolent questions. Besides, I much doubt whether you are admitted as a visitor to the house of Major Campbell, and even if your company should be tolerated, it cannot be as the lover of either Laura or Florence Campbell."

" There you are quite wrong," answered Paul, with a contemptuous sneer ; " for it so happens that the major and I have been upon pretty close terms of friendship for some time past. You seem to doubt me ; yet 'tis true, Stephen Harland ; and, as you do not seem inclined to heed my warning, I may presently be compelled to use force, when I thought a few words of advice would be sufficient to prevent any violence between us. I am not to be trifled with in a case like this ; and if you don't think proper to turn back, I shall be obliged to use force, that may end in bloodshed."

" Psha !" exclaimed Stephen, impatiently ; " this is a frivolous wasting of time that I cannot endure much longer. If you have any injury to complain of, state it briefly and honestly, that I may know exactly how the case stands between us. Of what motives do you suspect me ?"

" You have a sneaking kindness for a young lady that lives yonder," replied Paul ; " and as I happen to have been beforehand with you, it is my present design to warn you against visiting her any more ; and, if you refuse to take my counsel, it will then be for me to prove that I am not a man to be trifled with in a case like this."

" What reason," demanded Stephen Harland, " have you for suspecting that my motives are such as you have imputed to me ?"

" It matters not why I think so," replied the fugitive ; " and you must, therefore, rest satisfied with my declaration that I know such to be the fact. You have now heard, and, I suppose, can understand my meaning, without further parley."

" You seem to think I am as easily frightened as a child," returned Stephen ; " and it is therefore time that you should understand the person you seek to intimidate. My way lies straight before me, and it will be at your own peril to offer any further obstruction to my progress."

" We part not quite so soon," exclaimed Paul Rayland, as he moved a few paces on one side to stay the progress of the other. " It seems you are tolerably candid in your replies, so now tell me if your purpose in going yonder is to see Miss Campbell ?"

" I am going to see the family," answered the young man, with increasing impatience. " And now, having nearly exhausted my stock of good nature, I desire you to stand out of my path, that we may put an end to a meeting that has already lasted a great deal longer than I could have wished."

" You shall not leave me till I have said all that I intended," replied Paul, with dogged resolution. " The truth is, I love Miss Campbell ; her heart has been freely pledged to me, and, in spite of any obstacles that may be thrown in our way, she has promised to be mine. You, it seems, would cheat me of my prize, whilst it is yet within my grasp ; but, sooner than lose her, I will have the heart's blood of my rival."

" Dare you tell me," cried Stephen, " that Miss Campbell has ever been imprudent enough to promise her hand to such as you ?"

" I have told you nothing but the truth," answered Paul Rayland; "and though you may sneer at my good fortune, it is as true as that you now stand before me that Miss Campbell has promised to become the wife of him you affect to treat with so much scorn."

" I cannot—will not believe you," exclaimed the other. " This is a falsehood, intended to deceive me ; but never can I give credit to an assertion so improbable as this. Nay, from what I know of the whole family, they would loathe a man whose conduct, even within the last half hour, has proved that he is the associate of the lowest and most depraved characters."

" Beware how you urge me too far," returned Paul through his clenched teeth. " So far, I have kept my temper better than I had believed it possible ; but it cannot last much longer ; and if the fire should burst forth, it will not be checked till your insolence has met with its just punishment."

" You seek to intimidate me," answered the young man ; " but again I say I will not believe you have received encouragement either from Miss Campbell or her father."

" You can be convinced by asking her the question yourself," replied Paul. " She will tell you that we met frequently in London—that our vows to each other were there uttered—that her father knew of the love which had sprung up between us, and that, instead of discouraging my attentions to his daughter, he looked upon me with favour, and even seemed anxious that our union should not be delayed longer than necessary."

" And, even supposing you to have uttered nothing but the truth, I am to be debarred from entering the house of Major Campbell for no other reason than because it is your sovereign will and pleasure that I should be banished from the society of my friends. This is what I neither can nor will endure, and you may therefore spare yourself all further unnecessary trouble upon the subject."

" I shall, at any rate, take care to prevent your robbing me of one that is dearer to me than life," answered Paul. "She loves me, and whilst that certainty remains, I will endure no rival in her affections."

" You are a villain," exclaimed Stephen Harland, " or you would not seek to destroy the happiness of a too confiding girl."

" I am no villain," replied the other ; " or, at least if I am one, you shall not dare tell me so a second time."

" Then move on one side," exclaimed Stephen ; " for my object in coming forth to-day was to call at the house of Major Campbell, and I will not return till I have effected it."

" You are a fool for your pains," answered the fugitive ; " for I have known the major longer than you have, and I know him to be as great a villain as you believe me. Nay, more, his daughters are scarcely better than the parent under whose pernicious example they have been brought up."

" 'Tis false ! and thus do I punish the villain who would slander the pure and innocent !" exclaimed Stephen Harland, as he rushed forward and struck his more powerful adversary full in the face. Paul was so little prepared for this assault, that he reeled beneath the blow that had been dealt ; but, quickly recovering himself, he snatched a knife from his pocket, and, opening the blade, made a desperate blow at his antagonist. Stephen, however, suspected some such return for the violence he had used, and stepping back a couple of paces, he made what hasty preparation he could to protect himself from the fury he had thus excited. Thus guarded, the first attack of Paul was frustrated, but they instantly closed with each other in a death struggle, the result of which was for some few minutes doubtful. At length, however, Stephen received a wound in his side from the weapon of his antagonist, and a second thrust was about to follow when a loud shout was heard, and one of the gipsies springing forward parted the combatants, and, as he held Paul Rayland firmly in his grasp, called loudly upon the other to fly and save his life while he had an opportunity. For a moment Stephen paused as if scorning to seek safety by flight ; but his wound forbade any chance of renewing the conflict, and exerting what little strength remained to him, he left the place whilst his formidable antagonist was struggling to release himself from the hold of the man whose fortunate arrival on the spot had prevented the consummation of his villanous design. At last Paul broke away, and, blinded with rage, darted at his utmost speed in the direction that had been taken by his adversary; but scarcely had he proceeded a couple of hundred paces than he encountered Richard Elliot, who chanced to be travelling the same road, and whom he seized with a deep growl of exultation, under the supposition that it was the person of whom he was in pursuit. But the task he had now undertaken was one of greater difficulty than the former one, for Elliot was a robust, powerful fellow, and the chances were so much against the man who had made the attack that, by the time the gipsy came running up, Paul Rayland was completely at the mercy of his antagonist, and he would have perished by the very weapon that he had been the first to use, had not Rob dealt the victor a tremendous blow, that sent him reeling to the earth, where he lay completely stunned by the violence of his fall.

"Fool that you are!" exclaimed Rob to his companion, "must you ever be getting into these brawls that will, sooner or later, bring trouble on you? I have saved your life, and if you do not fly with me into the thickest part of yonder wood there will be worse come of this day's fray than in your madness you seem to expect."

"Lead me where you please, do with me as you will," muttered Paul, gnashing his teeth with mingled rage and disappointment. "You have thwarted me when my first antagonist was utterly at my mercy, and ——"

"Saved you when you were utterly at the mercy of the other," interrupted Rob. "You have much to grumble at, truly, Paul Rayland; but, perhaps, when you grow a little cooler you may begin to think that it was a fortunate chance that brought me to the spot just at the moment I came up. But it is no use talking here when an alarm has most likely been given in the neighbourhood, so come along with me and we'll find a place to hide ourselves in where those bloodhounds of the law shall have very little chance of finding us."

Paul offered no resistance to this proposition, but accompanied the gipsy without making any reply, and in a few minutes they had entered a thickly entangled part of the wood, where they might remain in concealment with little fear of immediate discovery. Shortly after their disappearance Richard Elliot began to recover from the effects of his severe fall; but so bruised was he that it was not without considerable difficulty he managed to raise himself from the ground. On looking about he quickly discovered that both his antagonists had disappeared, and, somewhat consoled at having been thus left to himself, he determined to return home without loss of time. This, however, was a task of greater difficulty than he had imagined, for he had received several severe contusions in his fall, and it was by slow and painful efforts that he at length succeeded in reaching his own door.

But the case was far worse with Stephen Harland, who was suffering from loss of blood to so great an extent, that it was only by the exertions of all his fortitude that he made his way towards the house of Major Campbell. On arriving there at last, however, exhausted nature could support him no longer,—a dizziness took possession of his brain, and he knew nothing more till his wandering senses once more returned, and he found himself extended upon a couch, with Major Campbell and his two daughters sedulously employed in effecting his recovery from unconsciousness.

Upon examination it was discovered that the wound he had received was of a mere superficial nature than had been anticipated, and by the application of proper remedies he was soon so far restored as to be able to describe the conflict in which he had been engaged, though he could give no information of his antagonist, who he had never seen till the moment of his encounter. Major Campbell soon afterwards left his daughter to attend upon their patient, and then Florence, whose anxiety had been excessive, inquired what sort of person it was that had wounded him.

" I can scarcely describe him," replied Stephen, " except that he was tall and of a swarthy complexion."

" Most likely it was one of the gipsies that infest the place they call the Haunted Hollow," observed Florence, somewhat relieved.

" On the contrary," answered Stephen, " he had the appearance of one who has moved in a superior station in life. There was a coarseness in his manner it is true, but it was evidently assumed for the purpose of deceiving me as to his real character."

" Alas, alas!" groaned Florence, unable to repress the agony she endured; " then are my worst fears but too dreadfully realized."

" Hush!" whispered Laura; " or you will betray a secret that will end in madness to us all. Say no more, dearest sister, lest you bring ruin upon one who has unfortunately obtained the mastery over your heart."

" Whoever the ruffian is," said Stephen, to whom these words had been inaudible, " I believe there is not much chance of his being discovered. He knows the danger of remaining in a neighbourhood that is no longer safe for him, and doubtless has left the place long before this time."

" It is to be hoped so," exclaimed Laura; " for should he be taken on a charge like this, he would be doomed to die the death of a criminal."

" He has nothing to fear from any vindictive feelings on my part," replied Stephen Harland; " for, desperate as was the attack he made upon me, I have reason to believe that he has excited the tender sympathies of those whose happiness is dearer to me than my own. I will pardon him the violence he has committed on me, but I trust chance will never again throw us in each other's way."

Here the conversation was interrupted by the entrance of Mr. Beaumont, who came with all haste upon hearing of the dangerous encounter in which his young favourite had been engaged. He was agreeably surprised on finding that the wound was not so dangerous as he had imagined, and half joking, half in earnest, he reproached Stephen for leaving home without saying whither he was going, or how long he should be absent.

" But we will say no more about it till you get well again, my dear boy," he added; " and so make yourself quite easy in the certainty that no trouble or expense shall be spared to bring the villain to the fate he deserves. I have already given information of the murderous attack made on you; and as a large reward is offered for his apprehension, I think we have every reason to believe that a very few hours will serve to put an end to all further danger from him, and even if we do not catch him, we shall still have reason to congratulate ourselves on driving him from the neighbourhood."

Stephen Harland assured his kind-hearted friend that the wound he had received was scarcely worth a moment's consideration, and in a short time he succeeded in changing the conversation into another channel. It was found, however, that Stephen could not be safely removed for some days to come, and as Major Campbell would not hear of his leaving the house till the wound was healed, Mr. Beaumont at last took his leave with a promise to visit the patient every day till he could return once more to the Manor-house.

CHAPTER VII.

My soul is changed,
Wronged, spurned, reviled—and it shall be avenged.—BYRON.

THE story of the murderous attempt that had been made upon Stephen Harland was quickly circulated through the neighbourhood, and instantly the whole population was roused and in active pursuit of the offender. Few, it must be admitted, felt very anxious to encounter a man whose recent daring attack upon Stephen was the theme of general conversation, yet, as a considerable sum had been offered for his apprehension, all parties were willing to run a certain degree of risk on condition of earning the promised reward.

Major Campbell found no great difficulty in guessing who was the author of the outrage, but there were reasons for maintaining the secret as long as possible, and as the happiness of Florence was in the scale, he determined to keep a careful watch over the actions of the reprobate, and, when a favourable opportunity arrived, to dismiss him for ever from the presence of his daughter.

Three or four days passed away, and as Stephen recovered from the effects of his wound, he became more and more delighted with the society of the two girls, and they became his almost constant companions in the strolls he took round the grounds belonging to the mansion, and Major Campbell, though at first scarcely enduring his presence, began to form a hope that he might bestow his affections upon Florence, and thus prevent her union with a man whose character was stamped with infamy. It seemed to him almost certain that Stephen Harland paid greater attention to Florence than to her sister, and so far there might be some reason to believe that he was not wrong in his conclusions; but, on the other hand, he well knew the romantic disposition of the younger daughter, and as she had once given her heart to Paul Rayland, there was much to fear that she would continue to love him in spite of the reckless course he had been pursuing for some time past. His chief dependance therefore was, that the fugitive would no more venture in the neighbourhood of the Clock-house, and in that case Florence might in time forget the object of her misplaced regard, and transfer her affection either to Stephen Harland, or some other person of equal worth and respectability.

Mr. Beaumont was indefatigable in his endeavours to discover the ruffianly assailant of his young favourite, yet though various schemes were tried for that purpose, they each failed in their turn, and to his no small dissatisfaction, he was obliged to acknowledge to himself that he had engaged in a project that was hardly likely to be rewarded with success. Angry at the defeat of his plans, he one evening presented himself at the mansion of Major Campbell, and throwing himself into a chair, gave utterance to the overflowing of his wrath in no very measured terms. Stephen well knew that argument was always thrown away in cases like the present, but having suffered him to exhaust his invectives, he ventured to suggest, that as his assailant had found it necessary to betake himself to a place of refuge, there was no probability of his ever venturing near enough to disturb their quietude again.

" But, sir, there is a probability, and a great one, too," answered the old gentleman, pettishly ; " and I'm afraid you will soon have reason to see that I am not wrong in my notions about this scoundrel. I'll be bound he has found a lurking place at no very great distance from here, and when the affair has blown over a bit he will venture abroad again, and then we shall see him make another attempt upon your life that may prove more fatal than the last."

" Then I will avoid him," replied Stephen, " and in doing so, I shall only pay a visit to London a little sooner than I had intended."

" Visit London !" ejaculated Mr. Beaumont, with surprise ; " and pray, sir, what do you think of going there for ?"

" To make my way in the world," answered Stephen, " by seeking out some honourable employment in which I may prove useful to my fellow men."

" A very romantic notion, truly !" exclaimed his patron. " And so I am to be left alone that you may put in practice some of the wild schemes that have entered that foolish head of yours."

" I trust," replied Stephen, " that my projected visit to London will not prove so wild a scheme as you imagine. In short, I am weary of living in idleness, and would fain employ what little talent I possess in obtaining the means to support myself in credit and respectability."

" Or, in other words, you are weary of an old man's society, and would now mix in the gaiety and frivolity of London life."

" Nay," replied Stephen ; " I am not ungrateful for the kindness and generosity you have manifested in my behalf, but there are reasons why I should adopt the course I have spoken of ; and you will, perhaps, admit that I am not unwise in leaving a place where I may be continually exposed to the secret attacks of a hidden foe."

"Why, there's some truth in that, to be sure," exclaimed Mr. Beaumont; "and if you had no other reason for leaving me, I might, after a little reflection, consent to a parting that must occasion me a good deal of pain. But you talked just now of entering some profession—may I inquire which one you think yourself best adapted for?"

"I have had thoughts of the army."

"Ah! I see how it is. You have been dazzled by the finery of a red coat, and would leave your best friends for the pleasure of wearing one. It's all vanity, sir, and, if my authority is worth anything you shall never enter the service, even though you were sure to become commander-in-chief."

"Have you the same objection against the navy?" inquired Stephen.

"A still greater one," replied the other; "for there you would be exposed to double danger of being slain in some engagement, or of going to the bottom in a hurricane. No, no, Stephen, take an old man's advice for once, and, if you must needs seek a profession, let it be one that will allow you to spend your days peacefully in England."

"It will be difficult to find one," replied Stephen, "for I am too old to think either of the church or the law."

"And if you were not, I should object to them both," answered Mr. Beaumont; "for, in the first place, you might turn out to be a consummate hypocrite, and in the second, an arrant knave. So we'll talk this affair over another time, Stephen, and, in the meanwhile, I hope you will think better of the matter, and remain beneath a roof that shall be a home to you as long as you think proper to accept its hospitality. As for this fellow that made the attempt upon your life, we must try to get him safe under lock and key, and then, if the laws are too merciful to hang him, we shall, at least, have the satisfaction of seeing the fellow sent out of the country for the remainder of his life."

Major Campbell and his daughters now entered the room, and the conversation was changed into another channel, in the midst of which Mr. Beaumont took his departure to wend his solitary way homewards. As he proceeded his somewhat ruffled temper became more calm; but again was it roused as he approached his own garden gate, near which, through the dim twilight, he could perceive two persons in secret conference, one of whom he discovered to be his servant Patty, and the other her libertine lover, Richard Elliot. The old man's blood boiled as he thought of the injury plotting against an inexperienced girl, and it was with difficulty that he could restrain himself from rushing before them. But second thoughts somewhat cooled him, and as he turned away in another direction, he heard Elliot propose another meeting in a place where they would be less likely to be watched or overheard.

On that same evening Florence Campbell secretly left her father's house, and taking an obscure path, directed her way towards the Haunted Hollow, where she thought it possible she might meet with Paul Rayland. Never till now had she felt so apprehensive of danger, and frequently did she pause with a half formed resolution to return home, but as often did she continue her way in the anxious hope that she might see her lover, or, at least, hear if he had succeeded in reaching a place of safety. At length she again paused as approaching footsteps were distinctly audible, and scarcely had she time to look around when a rustling was heard in the hedge by her side, and ere she could run from the spot the old gipsy woman stood before her.

"You have chosen your walk late, young lady," exclaimed the hag, "and the place is somewhat lonely for a maiden to trust herself in at this hour in the evening. But love prompts many a bold act, even in the most timid."

"I was merely walking for my own pleasure, good mother," answered Florence, with trepidation. "The day has been warm, and I came forth to ——"

"Meet one who shall be nameless," interrupted the gipsy. "You see, young lady, I know your thoughts,—ay, and can keep them secret, too, if you will only condescend to believe me your friend."

"If you are really so," cried Florence, "you will suffer me to pass on."

"Nay," answered the gipsy, "I should scarcely deserve to be called your friend were I to fail in the purpose that brought me hither."

"For Heaven's sake let me know your purpose?"

"It is to conduct you to one that you will be glad to meet."

"Ah! you mean Paul Rayland?"

"I do."

"Where is he?"

See page 28.

"It would be dangerous to answer your questions," replied the woman, "lest there should happen to be listeners about. A reward has been offered for his apprehension, and I may not utter the secret of his lurking place even to one who is so anxious for his safety as yourself."

"Is he far from home?" demanded Florence, irresolute whether to go with the old woman.

"Not so far as to tire you," replied the other; "so come with me, and I promise that before long you shall be in the presence of your lover. Follow me, gentle maiden, follow me, and I will lead you by an easy path to the spot where he is anxiously looking for your arrival."

"How can that be," demanded Florence, "when he knows not that I have left my father's house?"

The woman made no reply, but moved forward, and involuntarily the maiden followed, though not without glancing fearfully around her at almost every step, and sighing as she reflected on the imprudence that had prompted her to quit the protecting roof of her parent. At last they reached an open glade in the wood, and as the gipsy guide vanished, Paul was seen, by the pale light of the moon, approaching the spot to which she seemed fixed as if by the power of enchantment.

"So," he exclaimed, bitterly, "you have left my more favoured rival to come hither for the purpose of telling me that I am no longer loved. But I deserve the torture that wrings my heart, for he was within my reach but a few days since, yet did I suffer him to escape with a slight wound which your tender care has already nearly cured."

"This interview was scarcely expected, Paul," she replied; "and you might at least have spared me the reproaches that I do not deserve. I know not even to whom you allude as your rival, though I can but too well imagine you have grown jealous of the unfortunate young man whose life you sought, and who is at this time an inmate of my father's house."

"Ay, it is of him that I speak," answered Paul, "and my jealousy of him is founded on no slight foundation, or I should not have met him as I did for the purpose of ridding myself of a hated rival. And now what am I?—a wretched fugitive, for whose apprehension a reward has been offered by those who would gladly see him sent to the gibbet."

"Then why," demanded Florence, "do you not flee from the threatened danger?"

"Because I was resolved to seek one more interview," he replied. "Ever since the moment when I struck Stephen Harland to the earth I have been lurking about this place in the hope that we might meet together, and that I might hear from your own lips whether I am to be cast off as no longer worthy the love with which I was once honoured."

"Alas! and has it indeed come to this?" cried Florence, wildly; "do I indeed behold you a fugitive from justice, and for a crime, too, from which the souls of all good men revolt? But we waste time when you should be making your escape from a place where danger surrounds you—fly, Paul, fly, I conjure you, lest another hour should see you in the hands of those from whom you have no mercy to expect."

"Let it be so," exclaimed the other; "for even a death of shame would be better than a life of mortal agony. Till now, Florence, I have believed your heart was mine, and I thought to deserve your love by abandoning those evil courses that have made me execrated by my fellow men. But another has taken my place in your heart, and, goaded on by madness, I care not what act of desperation I commit in furtherance of the revenge I have sworn to execute. I will again see this Stephen Harland, and a second time he shall not escape me as he did before."

"Dear Paul," cried Florence, "there is no cause for this jealousy. The youth you speak of has never so much as hinted to me of love, and even if he had done so, I should have told him that my heart was already engaged. Ay, Paul Rayland, in spite of all that has happened, I am still faithful to you, even though the world hiss and point at me with the finger of scorn."

"It may be so," he replied; "but when suspicion is once roused, it is not easily to be removed. I am sure he loves you, and my only regret is that I did not slay him when the advantage was all my own."

"And thus," cried the maiden, "I should have lived to see you branded with the name of murderer—have heard your name execrated, and lived to know that you had expiated your crime on the gibbet. Think you, Paul, I could have endured all this without becoming mad?"

" Well," he replied, somewhat softened by her emotion, " I begin to feel that my jealousy was partly without foundation, and you must pardon the violence that had nearly ended in the death of Stephen Harland. The evil is done, girl, and the consequences, whatever they may be, I must endure. My foes watch for me on every side, so that I cannot escape, however willing I might be to try my chance, and it only remains for me to yield myself to them rather than endure this misery of suspense any longer."

" No, no," exclaimed Florence, with terror; " you may yet escape to some place of safety till this unfortunate affair is forgotten."

" That is impossible," he answered ; " for what little money I had is gone to bribe the gipsies who alone know of my retreat."

" And I," sighed the maiden, " have none with me at this moment to relieve your wants."

" It would be of little avail to me if you had," he replied ; " for all the people hereabouts seem to have made common cause against me, and a few hours, nay, perhaps a few minutes, will see me deprived of liberty, with but slight chance of ever being able to regain it."

" But have you not friends here among the gipsies ?" she demanded.

" I believed them so at one time," answered Paul ; " but I have lately observed indications that fill my mind with suspicion. They have heard of the reward that has been offered for my apprehension, and no doubt will surrender me to the officers of justice for the sake of the promised gold. At all events they know that I have parted with my last coin, and they have therefore no longer a motive for screening me as they have hitherto done."

" Then fly," cried the maiden, earnestly ; " fly, dear Paul, whilst a chance yet remains to you. I will remain faithful to the pledge I have given you, and should we ever meet again, I will no longer delay a union that you have so long urged."

" Will you be the companion of my flight?" he asked. " Say that you will be the companion of my flight, and from this moment I will abandon my evil life to become all that your fondest hopes can have pictured."

" It is impossible," she exclaimed; " such a step would drive my father to madness, and I cannot, dare not, leave my home, even though it be to follow you. But, hark, Paul ! what voices are those I hear sounding through the wood? It proceeds from a multitude, and I fear your pursuers are upon us, and that all retreat is cut off."

" Ay," he replied, bitterly, " the bloodhounds are indeed upon the right scent, and have surprised me when least I reckoned on their approach. Conceal yourself, dearest Florence, in this thicket, you may thus escape their vigilance, and at a favourable opportunity can return home without any one knowing of this interview between us. Farewell for the present, and do not forget that I shall return with what speed I can, to claim the promise you have vowed to fulfil.'"

Whilst thus speaking, he led her to the covert he had spoken of, and having once more charged her to be faithful to him, he dashed furiously away, and pursued a route opposite to that from whence the sound of voices came. Florence soon heard the men who had come in pursuit uttering oaths of rage and disappointment at the prospect of their search again proving a fruitless one, and it was not till long after the dead silence of night had been again restored, that she ventured from her place of concealment to return home with the same secrecy that she had quitted it.

With the first appearance of daylight, Paul Rayland crept stealthily from his lurking-place, and having first assured himself that none of his pursuers remained behind, he cautiously left the Hollow, and, almost unconscious of what he did, pursued the bye path that led towards the mansion of Major Campbell. Deeply musing upon his past adventures, and future prospects, he knew not that any one was approaching him, till a gentle voice roused him from his meditations, and raising his eyes, he encountered those of Patty, the rustic beauty, who had strolled out at this early hour to meet Richard Elliot, whose attention had won her guileless and unsuspecting heart. Deceived by the dim twilight, she had at first mistaken Paul for her lover, but no sooner was the error seen, than, with a cry of alarm, she would have fled away, had not the fugitive seized her hand, which she vainly tried to rescue from his grasp.

"Oh, sir! for pity's sake, let me go," she cried; "we are strangers to each other, and should we be seen together ——"

"Your lover would be jealous, and perhaps cast you off in anger," interrupted Paul. "It may be so, my pretty wench, but what of that? Are there not other lovers to be found in the world, that you should be so afraid of losing one who perhaps is not worthy the possession of so fair a prize?"

"I pray you, sir, do not detain me longer," cried Patty, entreatingly. "I have not sought this meeting, and if you are a gentleman, as your appearance would make me believe, you will suffer me to go my ways without further hindrance."

"You despise me, then, for a libertine who seeks your ruin?"

"Nay," she replied, "you wrong him most foully by calling him these names. He loves me, and that is more than you can do, seeing that this is the first time we have ever met each other."

"There you are wrong," answered Paul, "for I have seen you many a time when my presence has not been suspected. From the first I loved you, girl, but fortune has of late been so unkind to me, that I little thought an opportunity would ever present itself when I might tell you that my happiness is entirely at your own disposal."

"The greater the pity," returned the maiden, "since my heart is already given to one that I have every reason to believe deserves my regard. You have now heard me, sir, and I demand that you no longer keep me from an appointment that I would not willingly break."

"Go then," exclaimed Paul, as he released her hand; "go to your lover, and listen to the artful tales with which he will endeavour to add one more to the many victims who have already fallen beneath his libertine arts. But think not, girl, I am to be thus easily thwarted—I will hover round you, and it may be that ere long you will be forced to change this scornful tone for one of supplication, to the man whose offer you have rejected. Reflect on my words, and when next we meet, let me hear that you have dismissed this rival in my favour."

As he turned away, Patty fled with all her speed till she was met by Richard Elliot, who, half in jest, half in earnest, reproached her for keeping him so long after the hour of appointment. Panting as she was through the rapidity of her flight, she could not immediately reply to him, and ere she had stammered out an excuse, the approach of her master filled her with increased confusion.

"So!" exclaimed Mr. Beaumont, "this is just what I expected, and my presence may, perhaps, save a foolish, unsuspecting girl from the guiles and lures of a heartless libertine. I see, Patty, you are ashamed of the discovery that has taken place, and let me hope that you will no more trust yourself with a man whose baseness has prompted him to seek your destruction."

"You, presume, sir, on my respecting your age," cried Elliot, almost choking with anger; "but beware how you tempt me too far, or I may yet teach you that even old age cannot always command the respect I wish to show it."

"I am in no fear of your violence," answered Mr. Beaumont, calmly; "because I can yet wield a good stout cudgel with vigour, as you may hereafter have to acknowledge."

"And pray," demanded Richard Elliot, "by what right do you presume to interfere in an affair that you can have no business with?"

"By the right which every man claims to rescue innocence from villany," replied Mr. Beaumont. "This girl, though but an humble domestic in my service, is worthy of a better destiny than you seem to have proposed for her, and it shall be my care to guard her from the arts of one whose professions of love are as false as his own heart."

"How know you that I mean her wrong?" demanded Elliot, scarcely able to control his rage.

"By various unerring signs," answered the old gentleman. "The difference between your stations in life convince me that you have no honourable intentions towards her; the secresy with which your meetings have taken place would satisfy any reasonable man that you are ashamed of the world knowing of this love affair; and, above all, your character as a libertine assures me that her ruin is all you seek. And now, sir, having heard me, we will leave you to your own reflections upon the subject of our conversation."

He then bade Patty to return with him, and Richard Elliot was left to chafe at leisure over the castigation he had received.

CHAPTER VIII.

Ah! rather ask what will not pity dare,
When youth and pity lead like thee, Gulnare?—BYRON.

ON the day that Edward Cavendish obtained his majority, the whole neighbourhood was invited to partake in the hospitality with which the event was celebrated. Even the humblest cottagers were brought thither to meet their more wealthy neighbours; and, for that day at least, all restraint was thrown aside in honour of an occasion that diffused around a general feeling of joy. Tables were spread upon the lawn—the gardens were thrown open—musicians placed in various parts of the grounds, and, indeed, every preparation was made that might serve to gratify those who had been bidden to the feast.

Among the guests were Stephen Harland and his friend Mr. Beaumont—the latter of whom seldom mixed in what he called the frivolities of life, yet had been induced on the present occasion to honour the entertainment with his company. Major Campbell and his daughters were also there, and as Stephen's wound was by this time nearly healed, he walked about the grounds with Florence, and the attention he paid her became the subject of pretty general remark. Laura Campbell could not resist a sigh as, in imagination, she beheld the destruction of all her hopes, and she was still absorbed in her own melancholy thoughts when Edward Cavendish approached, and asked if she would accompany him in a walk among the promenaders. Laura silently assented, and had risen from her seat for that purpose, when the gipsy woman suddenly made her appearance, and dropping a low curtsey, inquired if they would like to hear their fortunes told.

"That will depend upon the nature of your predictions," answered Edward, laughingly. "If you have anything good to tell me, I can listen patiently, but I caution you to beware of giving utterance to words of evil import."

Half in jest, he gave her a piece of money, and as she took his hand, and examined the lines with great seeming attention, she exclaimed,—

"I can foresee much that you would be glad to learn, mixed up with a great deal that it would be displeasing to hear."

"Pshaw!" cried Edward; "then let me remain in ignorance, since I can put but little confidence in the predictions of an impostor."

"Be it as you please," answered the woman; "but there is one thing I would say, and that is, that your future destiny will be closely linked with the young lady by your side."

"That is at least satisfactory," replied Edward Cavendish; "since I can scarcely desire a greater source of happiness than to be associated with one whom I have long regarded with admiration and esteem."

"Yet your cup of happiness," answered the gipsy, "will not be without a full proportion of bitter in it. However, you have warned me against speaking of the darker side of your destiny, and I will, therefore, spare you the recital of it. Yet let me warn this young lady to keep a watchful eye upon one whose downfall has been plotted, and whose inexperience renders her an easy prey to the destroyer. He lurks around the house seeking the opportunity he desires, and a few days may bring sorrow and despair upon a heart that is too guileless to imagine villany can exist in one whose professions are those of honour."

"Your words terrify me, though I would fain pay no heed to them," cried Laura, with a shudder. "Leave me, woman, and let me hear no more foul slanders against those who are not present to confute them."

"What is it that has agitated you thus?" asked Florence, who at this moment approached them. "You tremble, my dear sister, but I can well imagine the cause, since the gipsy woman forms one of your party; doubtless she has uttered some foolish prophecy; yet, with all her boasted cunning, I'll answer for it that she cannot predict my fate, though I dare say it will be a peaceful one enough."

"Be not too sure of that," whispered the sybil, drawing her aside; "for when the wolf watches for the lamb, it is not easy to deprive him of his prey."

"You speak of Paul Rayland?" cried Florence, in a tone scarcely articulate from emotion.

"I do."

"Shall I ever see him again?"

"Ay."

"When?"

"To-morrow night. But beware of him, girl—beware of him, I say, lest you have bitter reason to repent that my words were suffered to pass unheeded."

Ere Florence could ask another question the gipsy had glided away towards another part of the ground. In the meantime Edward Cavendish had led Laura into the house, and feeling anxious to ascertain in what light she regarded Stephen Harland, he inquired how much longer he was expected to remain the guest of her father.

"I believe he quits us immediately," she replied, with a sigh.

"Have you not observed that he is somewhat changed of late?" asked Cavendish.

"He is more serious."

"Can you guess the reason, Miss Campbell?"

"I have scarcely given the subject a thought," she replied; "but, if I were to give an opinion about it, I should say that his altered circumstances weigh heavily upon his mind."

"You mean, I suppose," said Edward, "that he feels himself a dependant upon another since the death of the late vicar? I have myself thought his high spirit revolted from the kindness with which he has been received by Mr. Beaumont, yet surely that circumstance need not weigh upon his mind, since my house and purse are both at his command whenever he chooses to make a claim upon them."

"But, perhaps," answered Laura, "he has the same objection to accept the kindness you would generously extend towards him."

"There is no reason why he should regret such an offer made by me," replied Cavendish. "We have ever been like brothers together—were educated at the same college, and have since been upon terms of the closest intimacy. He knows the sincere friendship I have formed for him, and, perhaps, a word from you might prevail on him to accept the assistance that I know he needs."

"A word from me?"

"Pardon me, Miss Campbell," replied the young man, "if I have touched rather too closely upon a sensitive subject; but I cannot avoid seeing that you possess an influence over him that no other person can boast of."

"Indeed, indeed, sir, you are deceived," answered Miss Campbell. "I possess no influence over him, though I believe my sister has been honoured with the regard which you have imagined was bestowed upon myself."

"Would that it were so," exclaimed Edward; "for the certainty of such a fact would remove a heavy load from my heart."

"I think there can be no doubt of it," replied Laura Campbell, with a deep drawn sigh; "for since the accident which made him my father's guest, he has ever sought her society, almost to the exclusion of everybody else."

"And does your sister approve of his attentions?"

"That is a question I cannot answer."

"Perhaps," returned Edward, "it is one that I ought not to have asked, yet

I am about to put another that must appear equally impertinent ; in short, I would know whether your sister's heart is entirely at her own disposal ?"

" I would fain hope so," replied Miss Campbell, " yet I fear she has formed an attachment that, if persevered in, can only end in wretchedness and misery."

"In that case," observed Cavendish, " it is likely she will regret the offer of Stephen Harland in the event of his making one. But I see this subject distresses you, and we will now bring it to a close. My guests I hear are now assembling in the ball-room, and, if you will accompany me there, I will endeavour to compensate for my rudeness by touching no more upon this affair."

Laura took the offered arm of Edward Cavendish, and mixing with the happy throng of dancers, she soon forgot the subject which had engrossed so large a share of her thoughts. At an early hour Major Campbell and his two daughters left the scene of festivity ; but there were few among the visitors that felt inclined to follow their example, and it was not till three hours after midnight that the sounds of revelry and mirth ceased to be heard. The guests then began rapidly to take their departure, and Stephen, who had remained till the very last, was about to bid farewell to his host, when Cavendish, leading him to the refreshment room, said, as they seated themselves at a table,—

" You, at least, my dear friend, need be in no haste to leave me ; and now, like two bachelors, as we are, we will talk over a glass of wine, of certain matters that I would confer with you about. So, coming to the point at once, I ask what is your candid opinion of Florence Campbell ?"

" A somewhat singular question !" replied Stephen, with momentary surprise ; " but, since it has been put to me, I will own that I think her exceedingly pretty, exceedingly kind-hearted, yet, withal, rather thoughtless."

" Could you ever love her well enough to make her your wife ?"

" Humph !" ejaculated the other, " I have scarely ever given the subject a thought, yet, speaking seriously, I believe my regard for her would never arrive at that extent."

" Nevertheless," replied his friend, " I have a notion that she loves you."

" That may be," answered Stephen, " though, from my heart I hope you are mistaken, since no consideration shall ever induce me to seek as a wife one whose fortune, I have reason to believe, is very great."

" There you are in error," replied Cavendish, " for her prospects of fortune are very little better than your own. Her sister, Laura, inherits immense property from a relative, and hence, I suppose, occurs the notion you have formed."

" Are you sure of this ?" demanded Stephen Harland, with surprise.

" I am quite certain of it," replied his friend ; " and there is also reason to believe that her father, the major, is drawing pretty freely upon her purse to supply his losses at the gaming-table. She gives him with a liberal hand whatever money he demands, and, I fear, unless she shortly gets a husband, her present large fortune will go into the hands of her father's dissolute companions."

" Is there any probability of her marriage ?" asked Stephen, with a vain effort to appear composed.

" That, I believe, depends entirely upon yourself."

" Upon me ?"

" Ay," replied Cavendish ; " you have been bestowing all your attentions upon Florence Campbell, when, as I am a living man, the sister is pining away in hopeless love for you."

" Impossible !" exclaimed Stephen ; " she knows my poverty—that I am dependent on the charitable kindness of a friend—and never can she bestow her regard upon one who can have no claim upon it."

" Nevertheless, it is exactly as I have said," replied Cavendish. " I myself have had the presumption to aspire to her hand, but all hope is denied me since I have ascertained upon whom her affections have been bestowed."

" What ground have you for believing that I am so highly favoured ?"

" There are several reasons," answered Edward Cavendish ; " and this very night must have convinced me of the fact, even if I had not been tolerably certain of it before."

"Explain yourself."

"I will, and that briefly, too. Miss Campbell and I have had a long conversation together, in the course of which I endeavoured to ascertain what her feelings were towards you. I spoke of your seeming partiality for her sister,—the *ruse* answered even beyond my expectation—she trembled, her lips faltered, and such a deathlike paleness overspread her features that I verily believe she would have fainted, had she not been sustained by the thought that the secret of her heart would thus become known."

"Could I but be convinced," exclaimed Stephen, "that your surmise is correct, I should be one of the happiest fellows alive. But no, no; you are mistaken, Edward, and I must be mad to have yielded even for a moment to so vain a hope."

"My dear Harland, you must be blind not to have seen it yourself," replied his friend. "The girl cannot tell you that she loves, but surely you have had opportunities enough to see that your society is preferred to that of anybody else."

"Our acquaintance has been an exceedingly short one," answered Stephen; "and, till my accident rendered me the guest of her father, I never saw Miss Campbell more than half a dozen times in my life. In fact, I have thought her rather reserved in my presence, and on several occasions she has seemed to shun me."

"That was because you paid more attention to her sister than to herself," replied Cavendish. "She loves Florence dearly, and would sacrifice her own happiness rather than wound her feelings even in the slightest degree. So now tell me, Stephen, do you regard Miss Campbell sufficiently to seek her for a wife?"

"I do."

"And will you pop the question on the next occasion that offers?"

"Nay," he replied, "that I will not promise to do, lest you should have formed a mistaken opinion on the subject. To make her mine is the dearest wish of my heart, but to be met with a refusal would inflict so deep a wound upon my happiness that I dare not venture so far till I am well assured that my passion is returned with an ardour equal to my own."

"Then you think I am deceiving you?"

"Willingly, I am sure you would not do so," replied Stephen Harland; "but you may be mistaken in your surmises, and should that be the case my mortification would be extreme in the event of my being rejected."

"Ay, but there's no fear of it," exclaimed Edward Cavendish. "I was thoroughly convinced before I said a word to you upon the subject, and you may take my word for it that Laura will prove no coquette, though you, I am afraid, will be but a timid lover."

"My timidity," answered Stephen, "arises from a consciousness that I am unworthy the possession of so inestimable a prize as Miss Campbell. In truth, Edward, I scarcely dare to indulge a hope, lest disappointment should crush me beneath its weight."

"Psha!" retorted the other, "have I not told you there is no fear of disappointment? You will say, perhaps, that woman is a riddle, yet this one I can read correctly enough; and if you will not take my solution of it I can only pity you for a very foolish, headstrong fellow."

"But there is another reason that I have not yet mentioned," replied Stephen. "I have been received with kindness in the house of Major Campbell, when most I needed the hospitality that was so freely given, and it would be a base return on my part were I to gain the affection of his daughter when I have reason to believe he designs her for another."

"What do you mean, Stephen?"

"At present I cannot explain myself further," answered his friend, "because that which I have discovered has been the result of mere accident; I may, however, tell you that Major Campbell has a project to marry his daughter to some titled gamester, and I believe arrangements are already in progress for carrying the plan into immediate effect."

"All this signifies nothing," exclaimed Edward Cavendish. "The father may form what projects he pleases, but I am certain the young lady's heart is already given to you, and if her love is worth the possessing she will not consent to the match you speak of even though at the command of her parent."

See page 35.

"Then she will bring down upon herself his heaviest maledictions."

"Which will be of little consequence, since he cannot drive her penniless from his door," answered Edward. "Fortunately she has wealth at her own disposal, and can therefore brave the storm of indignation that her choice of a husband may give rise to."

"And can she be happy, think you," asked the other, "when she afterwards reflects upon the curses of an offended parent? Thoughts will intrude, even in spite of ourselves, and dreadful must hers be should she act in opposition to her parent, even though the command be harsh and oppressive."

"She can feel little uneasiness," answered Edward, "when she remembers that her father would marry her—in pursuance of his own designs—to an unprincipled gambler, whose coronet is tarnished by the course of profligacy he has followed. Major Campbell, I will admit, can boast the possession of some few good qualities, but in this instance he has been guilty of an act that in cooler moments he will feel ashamed of."

"Yet will be too proud to acknowledge it."

"Very likely he may be," answered Edward; "but at any rate he will in time be reconciled with his daughter's choice of a husband. Injure her he cannot, because in a great degree he is dependent on her for supporting him in the station he has hitherto enjoyed, so I dare say he will pocket the affront and become reconciled to his son-in-law, even though he does not happen to wear a coronet. However, I see my arguments have not yet made much impression on you; so reflect upon what we have been talking about, and when next we meet each other let me hear that you have conquered your diffidence, and will seize the golden opportunity whilst it is in your power to do so."

By this time daylight was beginning to dawn, and Stephen Harland took his departure. The conversation he had been engaged in occupied his thoughts as he pursued his homeward way, and ere he had accomplished half the distance he resolved on taking an early opportunity to broach the subject to Miss Campbell.

CHAPTER IX.

Sweet roses grace the thorny way,
Along this vale of sorrow;
The flowers that shed their leaves to-day,
Shall bloom again to-morrow.—MONTGOMERY.

DOUBTFUL as Laura Campbell had been whether she really possessed the regard of Stephen, she was still more so after the festival given by Cavendish, and her spirits became more oppressed than ever. With feelings somewhat akin to jealousy, she had observed the attention of Harland to her sister, and mortified by the reflections that forced themselves into her mind, she determined thenceforth to discard him from her thoughts, and by forgetfulness of the past, to regain the composure she had of late been a stranger to.

Nor was Stephen Harland less a prey to uneasy meditations after the conversation with his friend Cavendish, for in spite of the confidence with which the latter had spoken, it seemed impossible that Miss Campbell could have yielded her love to one whose fortune was well-known to be at the lowest ebb, and of whose birth strange rumours had been whispered for some time past in the neighbourhood. Still, however, he could not but acknowledge to himself, that such a union would be desirable, if she really loved him; and, after weighing the matter carefully in his mind three or four days, he at last resolved to pay another visit to the mansion of Major Campbell, and convince himself, if a chance should present itself, whether he was as much loved by Laura as his friend had represented. With a heart palpitating between hope and fear, he reached the Clock-house, and being well-known to the domestics as an acquaintance of their master, he was conducted to a room where he found Florence, who had just returned from taking equestrian exercise. As usual, she was full of life and gaiety, and, glancing her laughing eyes at him, she exclaimed,—

"So, sir, you have at length deigned once more to honour our poor house with a visit; had you come a little sooner, I might have had a companion in my ride, instead of galloping along the country without a male companion, except my groom."

" Had I known that my company would have been acceptable, Miss Campbell should not have had to reproach my want of courtesy," answered Stephen.

" Well," she replied, " that's tolerably spoken for one who is not remarkable for his gallantry. In short, sir, I am half inclined to forgive you, on condition that you take pity on my lonely condition in future."

" I thought," said Stephen, with hesitation, " there was another whose society you would prefer to mine."

" Then, indeed, are you mistaken," she replied, " for though it cannot be denied that I have been civil where civility has been first offered, there is no one whose company I prefer to your own. I know you will think me a bold, forward girl for saying as much, but the truth has been spoken, Stephen, though I must tell you at the same time, that what I have uttered is only as a sister might speak to her brother."

" Do you then regard me as a brother ?"

" Why, I may as well begin to do so now, as by-and-by," she replied; " for, unless my judgment deceives me, you are likely to be my brother-in-law before long. Ah! I have brought the blood to your face, I see, and you will hardly deny that I have spoken truly."

" I am afraid there is little chance of the happiness you speak of," sighed the young man.

" What! do you begin to despond already ?"

" I can see no reason to do otherwise," he replied. " My situation in life you are well aware of, and it would be the height of presumption to aspire where my heart assures me there is no prospect of success."

" That's spoken like all desponding lovers," answered Florence, gaily. " They are ever prone to look on the worst side of a picture, and must go moping about when they should be making themselves agreeable to the parties they wish to interest."

" Do you think I should have any chance with your sister ?"

" Now I must confess you have fairly puzzled me, because we women are rather apt to be tyrannical when we take it in our heads. That Laura does not absolutely hate you, I can take it upon myself to assert, but as she has never made me her confidante, I can only guess that you would not be very uncivilly received were you to speak boldly all you have to say."

" May I hope for your interest in my behalf ?"

" I possess but little that would be of service to you," answered Florence; " nor do I think it likely she would listen to any suggestion of mine. I just now proposed that you and I should ride out together—it would be an admirable plan to work upon her jealousy, and you would then see whether she really cares about you or not."

Before Stephen could make any reply to this, Laura Campbell entered the room, and from the angry flash that glanced from her eyes, it was easily to be seen that she was vexed at finding them in close and familiar conversation. She, however, quickly recovered her self-possession, and seating herself at the work-table, remained silent, as if communing with her own thoughts. Florence regarded her with an arch look, and then, as if without any particular object in view, she said,—

" I thought, dear Laura, you intended to have finished your picture to-day ?"

" I did so," she replied; " but the subject no longer interests me, and I shall therefore leave it for the present."

" No longer interests you !" cried Florence. " What! not the portrait of— of—you know who I mean ?"

" For Heaven's sake, sister, do not forget what you are speaking about!" exclaimed Laura, in alarm. " I have been foolish enough to trust you with a secret, and you would betray it, to my own shame and confusion."

" Nay, it was my own sagacity that discovered it," she replied, " or I should have remained in ignorance of the precious secret that you are so alarmed about. However, I can see no great harm in young ladies taking portraits of young gentlemen, so long as they keep the affair to themselves."

"It was done in a moment of thoughtlessness," said Laura, "and scarcely was the picture finished than destroyed."

"Very true," replied Florence, "but perhaps the original is no less dear because the shadow has departed."

"The original was never more to me than a friend," answered her sister, "and now can scarcely be called one. The portrait you speak of was drawn to fill up the vacancy of my idle hours, and never, perhaps, should I have remembered it again had you not reminded me of it thus unkindly."

"Are you angry with me?"

"I can scarcely be otherwise," replied Laura, "since you have chosen such a time as this to remind me of an act of folly that I feel heartily ashamed of."

"Then I have done wrong in speaking of the subject before Mr. Harland."

"You would have acted more wisely in never bringing it to my recollection," answered her sister. "I trust, however, Mr. Harland will excuse the thoughtless words of a giddy, foolish girl."

"Why I did not say the portrait was his."

Confused by these words, Laura rose from her seat, and with eyes filled with tears of vexation she hastily left the room. This was more than the kind hearted Florence could endure, and, leaving the couch upon which she had been sitting, she exclaimed,—

"I am indeed a foolish, giddy girl, as she just now called me, for I have vexed her to the very heart by the thoughtlessness I have given utterance to. But I must follow her and ask pardon for thus wounding her feelings. You will, I am sure, excuse me for leaving you so abruptly, Mr. Harland; and let me entreat you to forget, if you can, the words that I have uttered in the mere wantonness of a spoiled and over-petted girl."

She flew from the room as these words were uttered, and Stephen, lost in a labyrinth of thought, shortly afterwards left the house, scarcely knowing what construction to put upon the scene that had just occurred before him. There could, however, be no doubt that the portrait sketched by Laura was his own, and from that fact his vivid imagination painted the most flattering hopes. But, on the other hand, he discovered that the portrait had been destroyed as soon as finished, and the recollection of that circumstance served in some degree to cool the ardent thoughts that had found their way to his brain. At all events the discovery afforded him some little solace, since it was evident that he was not an object of indifference to Miss Campbell, and on reaching home he retired to the solitude of his own chamber, where he might, without interruption, pursue his own train of reflections, and form those plans which would be essential to attain the end he so fondly desired.

Since the festival given in honour of attaining his majority by Edward Cavendish, he had often reflected on the means by which he could serve his friend Harland, whose proud spirit, he well knew, would reject every pecuniary offer that he might make to him. The young heir now found himself wealthy beyond the expectation he had formed, and, strongly attached as he was towards his old playfellow and school companion, there was nothing that would have afforded him so much sincere gratification as to assist in raising him from the depression of fortune into which he had fallen since the death of the late vicar. But the difficulty was, how to break the subject to him, for he well knew the independent spirit of the man he would serve, and unless he proceeded guardedly in what his own good nature had suggested, there was little chance that his benevolent intentions would be carried into effect.

At last he thought of applying to Mr. Beaumont for advice; yet even there difficulties presented themselves that had not struck him at first. In fact, he well knew that the old gentleman, though, in reality, possessing an excellent heart, was a bit of a cynic in his way. There was a chance, therefore, that his motives might be misunderstood, and that it would be imagined he had some purpose of his own to serve, rather than to benefit the person in whose welfare he was so deeply interested. Still Edward was not to be deterred from an object upon which he had set his heart, and, after weighing the matter carefully in his mind, he took good heart and set forth to pay the old gentleman a visit.

On reaching the Manor-house, he found Mr. Beaumont walking in the garden, and was received more graciously than he expected. The old man had, at one time, been exceedingly partial to him, though their meeting had been very rare since the youth left the neighbourhood for college, and, smiling as he saw him approach, he inquired to what circumstance he owed the honour of this visit.

"But I can understand what you want with me," he added, after a brief pause; "you begin to feel the cares of life pressing upon you, and would ask advice from your elders, as every prudent man ought to do."

"I shall always esteem your advice, my dear sir," replied Edward; "but just now my own affairs require but little consideration. To come to the point at once, Mr. Beaumont, I desire to consult with you respecting my friend, Stephen Harland."

"Well, sir, well," exclaimed the old gentleman; "what have you to say about him?"

"You are aware that we were brought up together, and that we have ever regarded each other in the light of brothers."

"True; a romantic friendship formed in boyhood, that will be forgotten now that you have both reached the years of manhood."

"I trust not, sir," replied Edward; "at least I can answer for myself that I feel a stronger regard for him now than ever I did before."

"Humph! and you would have him live in the same house with you, I suppose," exclaimed Mr. Beaumont; "but it will never do, sir; the best of friends quarrel when they are too much together, and so, if you have any real regard for him, you will urge the subject no further."

"I have never entertained such an idea," replied Edward Cavendish; "and even if I had, I am sure the proud spirit of Stephen would never permit him to accept such a favour from me. Yet I would serve him, sir, and it must be through your means, or I have no chance of succeeding."

"To the point, sir; to the point," exclaimed Mr. Beaumont, impatiently; "if I understand rightly, you have found some romantic scheme for serving your young friend, Stephen Harland? Now, sir, let me hear your proposal as briefly as possible."

"In the first place, I need not tell you that he has been left destitute of fortune."

"Ay, ay; the boy's as poor as Job; and, to tell you the truth, I'm heartily glad of it."

"Glad of it, Mr. Beaumont!"

"To be sure I am," replied the old gentleman. "I have no family to provide for, and it shall be my chief gratification to provide for him, so that there shall be no fear of the poverty you seem to apprehend."

"Your liberality I do not doubt," returned Edward Cavendish; "yet perhaps I may be permitted to assist my friend, since it will afford me the greatest happiness to do so?"

"Pshaw! you talk like a young man that has had no experience in the world," exclaimed Mr. Beaumont. "You are lucky enough to have a large fortune, and must needs squander it away in utter thoughtlessness and folly."

"There can be no folly in assisting those whom we regard."

"So you think at the age of twenty-one," replied Mr. Beaumont; "but let as many more years be added, and your notions will be completely changed. Why, by that time you will have a wife and family about you, and that which you now talk of with so much earnestness will appear ridiculous and romantic in the extreme. I have had experience in that way myself, and can laugh at the folly which I would hold up as an example to you."

"But you have not yet heard my proposition."

"Then I will do so now, if you will only come to the point as soon as possible—proceed."

"I have been thinking, sir," began Edward, "that as my friend's means are very limited, the presentation of a few thousand pounds would serve to establish him in some honourable profession."

"A few thousand pounds!" cried Mr. Beaumont; "are you mad, that you talk of a few thousand pounds as if money was to be picked up in the kennel?"

"A small sum," replied Edward Cavendish, "would serve him in the way I wish."

"And a large one," exclaimed the other, "would make a thoughtless spendthrift of him."

"Not if he had your experience to guide and direct him," answered Edward. "He is not prone to the vices of the age, and if the means of starting were given him, I doubt not I should have the gratification of seeing him rise to eminence."

"So it seems, then, you would afford him the opportunity to quit the home that I have taught him to believe should be his so long as he thinks proper to accept of it."

"Far be it from me to interfere with any of your arrangements," replied Edward Cavendish; "for the only motive I have in making this offer, is to serve my friend."

"Which can most safely be done by permitting him to remain contented in his present station."

"Had I thought so, this offer never would have been made," answered the young man; "but I have reason to believe that Stephen Harland grows weary of his present situation."

"An ungrateful dog."

"Nay; ingratitude has nothing to do with it, nor can such a feeling harbour in his bosom."

"What else is it but ingratitude?" demanded Mr. Beaumont, "when a man turns his back upon those who are anxious to befriend him?"

"Stephen Harland regards you as his parent," replied the other; "but he is not without a feeling of independence; and I honour him the more for wishing to make his own way in the world, by following his own pursuits. He loves not a life of idleness and inactivity, but, if the chance were given him, would raise himself to eminence, in whatever course or profession he may happen to choose."

"Why, there I agree with you most cordially," exclaimed Mr. Beaumont; "for I have observed with no little satisfaction that he has perseverance enough to attain any object that he may set his mind upon."

"Then would it not be misdirected kindness on your part to frustrate such honourable ambition?" asked Edward Cavendish.

"Upon my word," exclaimed the other, "this is age being schooled by youth with a witness! But I like you all the better for what has passed between us, and your lecture has not proved quite so useless as I expected it would. You speak like a sensible fellow, Edward Cavendish, and though I seldom take advice from any one, I will not decide upon this affair till I have well reflected on it."

"Then I may consider it as a settled point, that Stephen will accept from me whatever sum of money may be required to establish him in the world?"

"That's more than I can undertake to say for him," replied Mr. Beaumont; "for he has an independent spirit of his own, and will most likely refuse your well meant offer."

"It is not my intention to make it myself," returned the other.

"How is it to be done, then?"

"Through yourself, if you will allow me to enlist your services in my behalf."

"Well," answered the old gentleman, "the subject requires more consideration than I can give it just now. But you have proved yourself a noble-hearted fellow, Edward, and though I'm not much in the habit of giving praise to my fellow men, I can't help acknowledging that you have found the right road to my heart."

"In that case I am sufficiently rewarded," answered the young man. "My motives towards Stephen Harland are actuated solely by friendship, and nothing can afford me such sincere pleasure as to hear from you, at our next meeting, that he has accepted the proposal. I would, however, wish that he should not know of the offer being made by me, as in that case it is not unlikely he would refuse to accept it."

" Would you have me base enough then," exclaimed Mr. Beaumont, " to tak upon myself the honour of doing this generous act ?"

" That I will leave entirely to yourself," replied the other ; " and if you think proper, you can tell him that an unknown friend of his has asked you to become a mediator in the affair."

" Ay, ay ; I must tell a good round lie, I suppose," exclaimed Mr. Beaumont. " But no matter, the cause is a good one, and I must blunder through it the best way I can. I don't expect he will listen to the proposition, however, so you had better not be too sanguine that your well intended offer will be accepted by your friend."

" In that case," replied Edward, " something else must be thought of, for I shall never feel half the enjoyment of my wealth unless it is shared with one whom I have ever regarded in the light of a brother."

" Very generous, upon my life !" exclaimed the old gentleman; " and I canno help adding, a little romantic too, since there are few people in the world who con sider themselves too rich. But you are inexperienced, and all I wish is that supposing Stephen should accept your offer, you will not afterwards repent your generosity."

" There is no fear of that," answered Edward Cavendish ; " the thought has occupied my mind for some time past, and I have only waited my coming of age to carry it into effect. At first I thought of making the proposal to him myself, but there was danger of a refusal, and so, at last, I determined to ask you to become the medium between us."

" The task is certainly pleasant enough," returned the other ; " and there is only one drawback, that I know of, to it. If he accepts the money he, of course, leaves my house, and that was a blow I was little prepared to sustain."

" But there will yet be a gratification," observed Edward, " in watching him rise to eminence through the talents of which he is possessed. He has industry enough to ensure success, and only needs our temporary assistance to make a figure in the world."

" Well," exclaimed the old gentleman, " I have yielded so far, Mr. Cavendish, as to promise that no obstacle shall be thrown in the way by me. I will draw him into conversation on the subject, and endeavour to learn which way his inclination tends."

" And of course," said Edward, " my name will not be mentioned ?"

" Depend on it I will take care that nothing shall escape my lips that shall in any way connect you with the affair," replied the other. " It will be taking all the merit of a kind act upon myself, it is true; but if he has half the sagacity I give him credit for, he will soon guess that the generous offer could have come from no person but yourself."

Thanking the old gentleman for his promised support, Edward Cavendish took his leave, well pleased at the success that had attended his mission. He felt entire confidence in the persuasive powers of Mr. Beaumont, whose influence over Stephen was unbounded, and there scarcely seemed to be a doubt remaining that the affair would terminate satisfactorily.

CHAPTER X.

I something do excuse the thing I hate
For his advantage whom I dearly love.—SHAKSPERE.

A FEW mornings afterwards, as Mr. Beaumont was sitting in the breakfast parlour, a servant entered to announce that a gentleman requested the favour of an immediate interview. On hearing the name of his visitor, the countenance of the old man assumed a clouded appearance, but this quickly gave way to his usual calm demeanour, and after a few moments' pause, he desired that the gentleman might be shown into the room. This order was promptly obeyed, and when the visitor approached, and the door was closed, Mr. Beaumont, addressing him as Lord Danebury, inquired to what circumstance he owed so unlooked-for a visit.

"My object shall be presently explained," answered his lordship; "but surely you cannot be surprised at seeing me, since this visit should have been long before this time."

"There were, no doubt, reasons for your absence," returned Mr. Beaumont, as he directed towards him a keen and searching glance.

"You must make allowance," said the nobleman, "for the mighty business that has deprived me of the command of my own time. I think it must be now upwards of twenty years since you and I saw each other last?"

"I dare say it may be, my lord," answered Mr. Beaumont; "but, with all due submission, I must request that you will come to the immediate object of your visit."

"I will. You are aware, of course, sir, that I have ever taken a deep interest in a youth named Stephen Harland?"

"Really, my lord, I was never aware of anything of the kind," replied the old gentleman.

"Nevertheless, it is so," continued Lord Danebury. "There is, in fact, a sort of doubtful relationship between us, and now that years are stealing fast upon me, I would ascertain his present situation in order that something may be done towards bettering his condition in life."

"Does such a proposition come from you, my lord?" exclaimed Mr. Beaumont, in a voice tremulous with emotion;—"from you whom I have met in deadly conflict, and whose blood has already dishonoured my sword? You ask for Stephen Harland. He is well, and needs no assistance beyond what I can afford him. You speak of him as being doubtfully related, and your words have raised thoughts of ire that I have long since tried to bury in oblivion. Beware, my lord, or an old man's anger may again be excited."

"Do you threaten me?"

"I wish only to caution you," answered Mr. Beaumont; "the youth you speak of is well."

"Where may I find him?"

"Under the guardianship of some distant relatives of his unfortunate mother."

"How can that be," exclaimed Lord Danebury, "when they cast her off as no longer worthy of their regard?"

"It is not my intention to enter into any explanation upon that point," replied the old gentleman firmly. "His protector will never surrender him to your care, unless proof be afforded of the right by which you claim him. Confess the infamy you have been guilty of—restore a fair name to the defamed dead, and Stephen Harland shall be taught to respect you as if no wrong had been perpetrated."

"Do you know," demanded his lordship, "to whom these insulting words are addressed?"

"Ay, too well!" replied the other. "Never can I forget your villany, and that we met together in mortal strife. You fell, mortally wounded as I thought, yet Heaven has spared you in its mercy to repent the foul wrongs you have committed."

"Nay," exclaimed his lordship, "surely, after the lapse of so many years, these things should be forgotten."

"By me they never can," answered Mr. Beaumont. "They live in my memory as fresh as if the occurrence was only of yesterday."

"Then let us speak no more of them," said Lord Danebury. "My errand here was a peaceful one; I came only to inquire where I may find this Stephen Harland."

"There is some scheme in this that you dare not explain," cried the other. "The child was deserted in his infancy, yet now you affect an interest in his behalf that I cannot give credence to."

"My motives are such as even you must approve of," replied his lordship. "News has reached me that his protector, the vicar is dead, and fearing lest he may have been left destitute, I came hither to inquire if he would accept a situation under government."

"In other words," exclaimed Mr. Beaumont, " you, who ought long ago to have dragged him from obscurity, would now generously procure for him a situation where he will be a fag to his inferiors. But he is not without friends, my lord, who will do something better for him than you propose."

"Do you dispute my privilege?" demanded the nobleman.

See page 55.

"Not I, my lord," replied Mr. Beaumont ; " but those will who befriended the youth when deserted by him who should have been his protector."

"It is vain to utter these criminations after the lapse of so long a period," exclaimed the nobleman. "Let it suffice that I am now anxious to better his condition—a situation will soon be open for him in which he may rise by his own merits and application."

No. 7.

"In other words, shame has at length overtaken you, my lord, and you would provide him with the means of existence, though not from your own purse. Lord Danebury, I can read your heart and despise you."

"Will your hatred of me never relent?" exclaimed the other; "and must this young man suffer all the evils of poverty because you cannot forgive an indiscretion committed in my youth?"

"You have never sought to make any recompense for it," answered the old gentleman. "Thanks to the care of strangers, Stephen Harland has never suffered through your heartless desertion. He has found protection, and will one day or another possess a fortune that even the proud Lord Danebury might covet."

"Who are the friends you speak of?"

"You, my lord, have forfeited all right to question me upon the subject."

"Tell me," exclaimed the nobleman eagerly; "is the secret of his birth known? Has my name ever been brought in question as being connected with this youth?"

"She who lies in yonder churchyard," answered Mr. Beaumont, "cannot betray the secret that festered in her heart till death. Thus far I have not uttered a word explanatory of the fatal truth, but how much longer my tongue will remain mute, depends upon yourself."

"Has the boy himself any notion of the facts respecting his birth?"

"He has not."

"When can I see him?"

"Perhaps never; he is happy, my lord, and your regard for him cannot be so great that you can have any real desire for an interview. The friend who has hitherto taken an interest in him will never relax in his duty, and, as I have said before, the time will come when Stephen Harland will have wealth and power at his command."

"It is evident that, for purposes of your own," exclaimed Lord Danebury, "you intend to keep me in the dark upon this subject. At present, I shall take no violent means to compel a disclosure, but will content myself with requesting you to tell the youth that I feel an interest in his welfare, and shall be ready to serve him with my interest whenever he may think proper to request it."

"I will deliver any message you choose to entrust me with," replied Mr. Beaumont; "but let it not be forgotten that it may lead to a discovery of his unworthy father, and then judge, my lord, what his feelings will be when he hears the narrative of heartless villany that has been perpetrated against him. Will he not curse his unnatural parent, and shrink from him as he would from the presence of a venomous serpent?"

"You would frighten me from my purpose," exclaimed Lord Danebury; "yet, be the consequences what they may, my purpose shall not be thwarted. Tell him the offer I have made, and invent any subterfuge you please to hide the reason of my interest in his behalf. To you I entrust the management of this business; and, for the youth's sake, I hope you will keep a secret that, if known to him, can only end in the misery of one that you profess to regard."

His lordship rose from his seat, and, bowing haughtily, disappeared from the room. In another minute or two he was in his carriage, and ere half an hour had elapsed he had reached the Clock-house, and was in close conference with Major Campbell. The visit was so unexpected that Campbell was at first puzzled to understand the motive of it, but soon after the greeting and welcome were over his lordship deigned to give his own explanation on the subject.

"You are surprised to see me, major, I dare say," he exclaimed; "but the truth is, I have no particular purpose in this visit, further than that I found it necessary to seek retirement at the close of a very heavy session; with your permission, therefore, I shall remain your guest for a few days, and we may, in the course of that time, complete certain little arrangements that have been talked over between us."

"Your lordship is welcome to my humble abode," exclaimed the major; "though I am afraid you will find it but a dull one after quitting the gaieties of the metropolis."

"You have a couple of daughters whose society, I am sure, will dispel ennui," replied Lord Danebury. "Laura is a delightful creature, and her presence will more than console me for leaving scenes of revelry that I begin to grow heartily tired of."

"And Florence, though you know her not so well, is greatly admired throughout the county," exclaimed the father. "She has more vivacity than her sister, and there are many persons who give her the preference."

"I see how it is, major," exclaimed the nobleman, with a chuckle at his own fancied penetration, "you have other views for the elder daughter, and would fain persuade me to choose the other one; but my mind is made up, I tell you, and either Laura must be mine or there's an end of the matter at once."

"Indeed, my dear lord, I had no thought of the kind," replied Major Campbell; "for it matters not to me which of the girls you marry, so that I have the honour to become your father-in-law."

"Ah! the coronet has dazzled you, then," exclaimed the other, laughingly. "You cannot resist the temptation of a title; and, between ourselves, Laura Campbell will grace her new honours admirably."

"Doubtless, my lord; doubtless she would," cried the major. "Laura is much admired for her beauty, and if I ventured just now to speak in favour of her, it was because she is of a livelier temperament, and, as a companion, is far superior to her sister; yet Laura is the steadier girl of the two, and I cannot help complimenting your lordship's taste in making the selection."

"Are you aware," asked Lord Danebury, "whether there is any rival in the way?"

"I rather think not."

"Do you ever have any young male visitors in the house?"

"There is one who occasionally comes to see us," replied Major Campbell; "but if he gives a preference to either of the girls, I rather think it is in favour of Florence. At all events, he seeks her society most, and I have never observed anything in the conduct of Laura that would lead me to believe she cared about him."

"That I shall very soon discover," said his lordship. "Of course the young man and I shall frequently meet together while I remain here, and if it should appear that his attentions are paid to Laura, I shall take steps for preventing his carrying off the prize."

"You will not get into a quarrel with him, I hope?"

"Why that will depend upon circumstances," answered the nobleman. "I don't wish to inflict personal chastisement upon the young fellow, but he must not irritate me, or there's no saying where the matter will end."

"I suppose, then," observed Campbell, "your lordship is quite determined upon a second marriage?"

"To be sure I am," he replied. "I have grown weary of remaining a widower so many years, and have thoughts of relinquishing the active duties of public life that have so long occupied my attention. I shall, therefore, require the society of a wife, and from what I have seen of your elder daughter, I pronounce her to be the very woman, of all others, to render this dull earth of ours a paradise."

"Does your son know anything of your intention?" asked Major Campbell.

"I neither know nor care," answered his lordship. "Besides, he is in ill health, and I have great doubts whether he will recover. A second marriage may bring me another heir, major, and there will be some gratification in preventing the title going to a branch of the family that I absolutely hate."

"And Laura is positively the choice you have made?"

"She is; and I suppose there is no reason to fear any opposition from you?"

"My lord," exclaimed Major Campbell, "the honour is too great a one to be thrown away for any trivial cause. Laura has ever been a dutiful child, and I feel certain she will accept with gratitude the proposal you have been pleased to make."

"She is a charming creature, and I am sure our tempers will agree admirably," said Lord Danebury. "But she may take it into her head that there is too great a difference in our ages, and, in that case, I suppose you possess sufficient power over her to compel submission."

"My wishes have ever been a law to her," replied the father; "and I apprehend no danger of a refusal, when she knows it is my wish that she should become Lady Danebury."

"Besides," added his lordship, "a title has attractions that few women can resist; she will overlook a little difference in years, and, lest any change should take place in her opinions upon the subject, the marriage must take place as soon as we gain her consent. She will be happy enough when she finds herself in the new sphere to which I shall introduce her; and who knows but the marriage of one daughter to a nobleman may lead to equal good fortune with the other?"

"I have said," observed the major, "that I rather think the affections of Florence are given to a young man who frequently visits here."

"Pooh! what matters that, if you can do better for her?" demanded Lord Danebury. "What's the use of being a father if you cannot make your children do as you please? Young folks never know what is best for them, and it becomes the duty of older ones to supply them with some of their experience."

"But I rather think Florence is not to be so easily managed as her sister."

"Yet just now you would have recommended me to marry Florence."

"Very true, my lord," replied the major; "but that was because I feel certain she will make an excellent wife. As for the young fellow who has been dangling after her, he might easily be got rid of—and should have been, too, if your lordship happened to give her the preference."

"You are extremely accommodating, I am sure,' exclaimed Lord Danebury, with a half sneer. "However, my choice has fallen upon Laura Campbell, and as it may be as well to act with candour, I will tell you why I have come to this conclusion. The truth is, your elder daughter has considerable property of her own, which will save me the mortification of bringing a beggar into my family."

"But perhaps," said the major, " her fortune is not so large as you expect."

"That's likely enough," replied Lord Danebury, "for I have heard it whispered that you have frequently borrowed large sums of money from her to make good your deficiencies at the gaming table. Nay, do not look so glum about it, major, for I have not heard it as a general report, but from one who is pretty deep in your secrets. To me this trifling loss will make no great difference, but, should she marry any other man, he might be too inquisitive in the matter, and require the amount to be refunded."

"Which I should find some difficulty in doing," returned the major, scarcely knowing what he said.

"And in that case," resumed his lordship, "your character might be ruined by a full disclosure of the whole transaction."

"Do I understand," asked Campbell, "that, in the event of your marrying Laura, I shall not be expected to replace the money I have borrowed of her?"

"Precisely so."

"Your generosity exceeds my expectation!" exclaimed the major. "Laura shall hear the noble sacrifice you are prepared to make, and that circumstance alone will, I am sure, win for you her gratitude and love. I have been thoughtless, Lord Danebury, and have not hesitated to reduce the fortune of my child in the pursuit of blind infatuation. But it has taught me a lesson that it is to be hoped will not be thrown away."

"It's all very well to say so," replied the nobleman; "but experience has proved to me that the habit of gaming is not to be so easily cast off as you seem to imagine. The only thing to be said in your favour is, that your chief resource will be gone on your daughter's marriage, and no gamester will be found to trust you afterwards."

"Spare me, my lord, I entreat!" exclaimed Major Campbell, "and do not add bitterness to the pangs I already feel. My daughter only guesses the cause of my temporary embarrassment—may I request it as a favour, that you will not further explain the folly her parent has been guilty of?"

"I am no tale-bearer," answered his lordship; "and even if I were, it is hardly likely I should speak to the prejudice of one with whom I am about to be so nearly connected. Whatever the fortune of your daughter may be, it shall be settled upon her, and I will add to it such a sum as shall support her in affluence should she out-live me—which, by-the-bye, is likely enough, seeing that she is some five-and-twenty years younger than myself."

"Then you have quite resolved upon the union of our families?"

"I had no other motive for paying you this visit," replied his lordship. "The subject has been uppermost in my thoughts ever since you and I last spoke of it, and now the increasing illness of my son has confirmed my resolution. You, it appears, have no objection to raise, and it therefore only remains with your daughter to pronounce whether she will reject or accept my proposal."

"There is no fear of her refusal," answered the major; "for I have always found her ready to sacrifice her own wishes to accommodate mine. Besides, I see no objection that she can possibly raise; her heart, I believe, is disengaged, and the honour of such an alliance is too great to be thrown away from mere humour or caprice."

"That remains to be proved," observed the nobleman; "for she may take it in her head to choose a younger husband, even though he may not happen to possess a title—which, between you and me, major, all women are not particularly anxious for. Miss Campbell may be one of those quiet, unpretending ladies; and in this event, down go all our castles in the air, and I may return to Danebury Castle to sigh over my disapppointment, or look elsewhere for a partner in my honours. But I will detain you no longer—go, seek your daughter; tell her the object of my visit, and try your best to obtain for me such a reception as I desire."

Major Campbell left his lordly guest to seek his daughter, whom he found in the room which they usually occupied in the morning. With a few preliminary observations, he introduced the subject of Lord Danebury's arrival, and after expatiating on his various excellent qualities—not one of which he could lay claim to—he came to the subject that had induced him to become a visitor at the Clock-house.

The announcement was heard with different emotions by the two girls: Florence was rejoiced that her sister was likely to form so high a matrimonial engagement, and she could not refrain from giving way to the rapture the announcement afforded her. Laura, however, heard her father with an intensity of anguish that she could not conceal. She saw the utter wreck of all her hopes with respect to Stephen Harland, and it required all her fortitude to suppress the tears of sorrow that were ready to burst from their fount.

She, however, uttered no word of denial, and this being taken as a sign of assent, his lordship was introduced with an assurance, on the part of her father, that matters were progressing well. The news was soon spread among the domestics, by whom it was reported in every direction, and in a day or two afterwards it was rumoured that a marriage was to take place between Miss Campbell and Lord Danebury.

CHAPTER XI.

You do not know this man—I do.
He's mean, deceitful, avaricious. You
Deem yourself safe, as young and brave; but learn,
None are secure from desperation, few
From subtlety. *We ner.*

THE current news of the neighbourhood soon came to be known to Stephen Harland, who keenly felt the blow that had thus been aimed at his happiness; and, in the utter despondency of his heart, he remained within doors for some days, notwithstanding the remonstrance of Mr. Beaumont, who could not imagine the reason of his young friend's sudden alteration of manner.   From one or another, Stephen heard all that took place at the mansion of Major Campbell; and as each piece of information served more and more to confirm the fact of a marriage being projected between Laura and the noble visitor, the lover could no longer restrain his petulance, and one morning when he and Mr. Beaumont were alone, he exclaimed, with a peevishness that was not usual with him,—

"It seems, sir, that this Lord Danebury is well satisfied with his present quarters, for though he has been at the Clock-house better than a fortnight, there are no more preparations for his departure than there were on the first day of his arrival."

"And pray what do you infer from all this?" asked the old gentleman.

"That the old fool contemplates marrying one of the major's daughters."

"Pray, which one," demanded Mr. Beaumont, "has the honour of winning the regard of a man old enough to be her grandfather?"

"The elder one, sir."

"Ah!" exclaimed the other, "then I must give his lordship credit for judgment. Laura was always my favourite, and it must be confessed I could have wished her a better fate than to become the wife of that man!"

"You know him, sir?" cried Stephen, hastily.

"Yes—no—that is, only by report," answered Mr. Beaumont, checking himself.

"And you know enough of him to wish that Miss Campbell was not likely to be his wife."

"I have heard things to his discredit," answered the old gentleman; "but, of course, we must not put too much faith in idle rumours.   We may, however, rely on the prudence of Laura, who will not throw herself away upon this man for the sake of a title, unless she is convinced that he merits the possession of her hand."

"I have thought so myself," replied Stephen; "but still his lordship remains, and a regular courtship seems to be going forward.   Major Campbell, I believe, is in some way or other under obligations to him, and being rather pressed in his pecuniary affairs, he is urging a marriage that I fear will end in misery to the intended bride."

"But the young lady has a voice in the matter, I should suppose."

"She has, sir," returned Stephen Harland, "but hesitates to dismiss her lordly lover on her father's account.   Thus she will become a victim to the madness that has urged her father to become a frequenter of the gaming-table.   She may wed him, but I am convinced her heart never can be his."

"And supposing all this to be true, why need we trouble our heads about it?" demanded the old gentleman.   "Marriage makes fools of a great many, and Miss Campbell has no more right to be exempt than anybody else."

"Yet we may surely regret the probability of her being unhappy."

"It will be time enough to be sorry when the fact is ascertained," replied Mr. Beaumont.   "Who knows but the girl may disregard a husband's coldness and neglect in the round of gaiety she will be introduced to?   The heart grows callous in time, and if the tempers of these people don't agree, they can part, as a great many have done before them, and there will be an end of the matter."

"But this Lord Danebury is no stranger to you," exclaimed Stephen; "I have reason to believe that you know something to his prejudice, and if so, I adjure you by every honourable feeling to warn Major Campbell against a marriage to which he is urging his daughter."

"Ay, I do know him," replied Mr. Beaumont, with vehemence.   "Know him for a villain—for a—but why do I thus inveigh against one whom I have long since tried to forget?   You ask me why I do not warn Major Campbell against the wretch that seeks his daughter's hand?   'Tis well urged on your part, Stephen, and I will do it.   This haughty noble has thus far gone on with impunity, but let him beware, for my vengeance is aroused, and he shall be made to feel that there is one who may yet triumph over him.   But leave me, Stephen, I would be alone.   By-and-bye I shall have recovered myself, and we may then speak further on this subject."

"I will go to the Clock-house," said the young man; "it is some days since I have been there, and I should like to witness the courtship of this titled dotard."

"Let no words of anger pass between you," exclaimed Mr. Beaumont, with alarm. "Remember, he is older than yourself, and if you must hate him, let the hatred be such as a son would bestow upon a father who had heaped upon him every wrong that his evil nature could conceive."

"Rely on it, I will seek no quarrel with a man for whom I can only feel scorn," replied Stephen. "I may not happen to see him, but, at all events, I shall hear what chance there is of his marrying Laura Campbell."

He then left his generous benefactor, and quitting the house, hurried across the fields, thinking all the while of the rival who was trying to supplant him, and reproaching himself for not having asked the hand of Miss Campbell when it would have been in her power to bestow it on him. On entering the Clock-house, he found Florence alone, and almost before the first salutation was over, she began to scold him with feigned anger for having absented himself so long.

"Indeed, Florence," he said, "I should not have done so, but that I thought the arrival of your titled guest would render my future visits unwelcome."

"Ah! jealous already," she said, smilingly, "and yet, perhaps, it is scarcely to be wondered at, for you have been like a spoiled child among us, and now you think our favour has been bestowed elsewhere."

"And is it not so?" he asked.

"How can you ask such a question?" cried Florence. "His lordship is certainly endeavouring to carry the heart of my sister by storm, but is that any reason why you should be less welcome than formerly?"

"I trust not," said Stephen; "but now tell me of this love affair—is your sister likely to accept the proposal of this lordly lover?"

"That is more than I can dare answer for," she replied. "His lordship is very assiduous in his attentions to Laura, and she, on her part, is so dutiful a child, that she would consider it a crime of the deepest magnitude to disobey her parent, even though her own future misery should be the consequence."

"And will her father be cruel enough to insist upon her making such a sacrifice?"

"My father says very little about it," replied Florence, "and seems to let her follow her own inclinations. She, however, well knows his wishes upon the subject, and so I dare say she will consent to become Lady Danebury, though I know she has not a spark of ambition to wear a coronet. But here she comes with her ancient lover, so of course you must endure an introduction to him, and must conduct yourself with as much civility and politeness as you can show to one whom you regard as a sort of rival."

Florence had scarcely finished speaking, when Laura entered the room, leaning on the arm of Lord Danebury. She appeared confused at seeing him; the colour left her cheek, and quitting her support, she threw herself into a chair, as if unable any longer to sustain her trembling limbs. Stephen would have hastened to her assistance, but Florence, foreseeing an awkward predicament, stepped forward and introduced him to the nobleman. Lord Danebury started as he heard the young man's name pronounced, but recovering himself, he said, with an effort at composure,—

"I have heard your name mentioned with favour, sir, as having carried off all the honours of the university. You have acquired fame early, young man, and it therefore appears singular to find you wasting your talents in an obscure place, where the hard labour of years is buried and forgotten."

"It may appear so," answered Stephen, drily; "but in this obscure place I have found friends, and hence my partiality to it. Among the foremost of these, my lord, is Mr. Beaumont, with whom, I believe, you are acquainted."

"I remember such a name," replied Lord Danebury; "he is, I suppose, related to you?"

"Not in the most distant manner," answered Stephen Harland; "but he is a friend to whom I am bound by the strongest ties of gratitude."

"If he is the person I mean," said his lordship, after a pause, "we knew each other many years ago on the continent, and the thing which most impresses the recollection on my mind is a love affair, in which he was involved, and which created a great deal of conversation at the time. By-the-bye, he made himself rather ridiculous, and many a laugh was uttered at his expense for the course he thought proper to adopt."

" I presume your lordship alludes to a duel in which he was engaged."

"I do."

" Then the laugh was rather against his antagonist, if I have understood rightly," said Stephen Harland, warmly, " for he was worsted in the encounter, and narrowly escaped with his life."

" I know very little about it," said Lord Danebury, with assumed apathy ; "and even that little is only through common report."

" At all events," exclaimed the young man, " you can never have heard any evil of Mr. Beaumont, who has ever borne the highest character for honour and bravery. The duel you speak of was occasioned by the villany of a supposed friend, who ——"

" Has he, then, made you fully acquainted with the facts ?" interrupted his lordship, hastily.

" I have heard merely the bare outlines," replied Stephen, " and have not even been informed of the name of his antagonist. It seems, however, that the wound was a serious one, and so far the punishment was richly deserved."

Lord Danebury remained silent with rage, and it was some few minutes before he could recover himself sufficiently to resume. At length, in a tone of apparent kindness, he said,—

" I have been thinking, young man, that your residence in this place is much to be regretted, since you have abilities that would give you a high station in society if they were properly brought out."

" Your lordship is very considerate," replied Stephen, with marked emphasis, "but I have an able counsellor in Mr. Beaumont, to whom I refer all such matters."

" You are fortunate in having such a friend," returned the nobleman, appearing not to observe the sneer. " I dare say Mr. Beaumont acts the part of a parent to you, but unfortunately he possesses very little influence that can prove serviceable. I, on the other hand, am closely connected with one of the ministers of the crown, and if you think proper now, or at any other time, to accept my offer, you shall have the first lucrative situation that happens to be vacant."

" I am obliged to you, my lord," answered Stephen Harland ; " but at present I have not made up my mind what course to pursue. I have reason to believe, however, that Mr. Beaumont has a scheme in view for me, and it would therefore be treating him with disrespect were I to accept your offer till I have ascertained whether his plans meet with my approbation."

" Besides," interposed Florence, " it is not to be endured that Stephen Harland should be taken away from us just as he is becoming such a prodigious favourite. I, for one, shall protest against it, and I am sure my sister will not hear of his leaving the neighbourhood."

" Your sister can feel very little interest in him now," said his lordship, with haughty severity.

" But others may, I suppose," exclaimed Florence ; " and if I was the young gentleman, I would see all the situations at Jerico before I would leave a place where I was respected by all the men, and adored by all the girls."

" Fie, sister, fie !" cried Laura, reproachfully ; "your thoughtless vivacity will give his lordship but a strange opinion of you, I fear. Stephen—that is, Mr. Harland, will, of course consult his own interest, which he cannot do if he remains in this place, where, according to his own words, he is in danger of being spoilt by the over partiality of his friends."

" Spoken like a sensible girl," exclaimed Lord Danebury ; " and if the young gentleman is not too proud to take good advice, he will act upon the hint, and accept my offer, without consulting any one upon the subject."

"Really," cried Stephen, "the extraordinary interest your lordship takes in my affairs seems to me most strange. Our acquaintance has scarcely existed a quarter of an hour, yet I have a proffer of your services as if we had known each other for years."

"It's always my way, young sir," replied Lord Danebury. "My impressions are formed upon the instant, and if I take a liking to any person I never rest satisfied till I have given him substantial marks of my esteem. I need not say that you have interested me in your favour, and the proposition that has been made was given in the most perfect friendliness."

See page 60.

Stephen's reply was interrupted by the entrance of a servant, with a message from Major Campbell to Lord Danebury, requesting to see him immediately in his study. A slight frown passed over his lordship's brow at the idea of leaving his intended and Stephen together; but he could not refuse the summons without betraying his own jealousy, and as Florence would no doubt remain with them, he left the room, though not without evident reluctance. Almost as soon as he was gone, Florence also took her departure, and then Laura, to her no small discomfiture, found herself left *tete-a-tete* with the man whom she still loved, but from whom she was to be severed by a cruel fate. Stephen was no less confused at a circumstance so unlooked for, but the opportunity was too favourable to be thrown away, and breaking the silence that had been kept between them, he said diffidently,—

"May I presume to ask, Miss Campbell, if the addresses of Lord Danebury are agreeable to you, or whether they are permitted in deference to your father's wishes?"

"The question is a singular one," she replied, "and I know not whether I ought to answer it. I will, however, be candid with you, Stephen, and confess that my heart never can be his lordship's, though I may give him my hand. My father's present circumstances require the sacrifice, and it shall be made, whatever the consequence may be."

"But surely Major Campbell cannot know that this projected match is opposed to your own wishes."

"I have been careful to keep that from him," she replied. "He anxiously desires to bring the match about, because it will relieve him from a load of anxiety that weighs down his spirit; yet he loves me, Stephen, and would endure anything rather than urge this hated union, if he knew how much I dread becoming the slave of this imperious lord."

"Will you then suffer me to be a mediator?" asked Stephen Harland. "Your father will not, I am certain, be offended at anything I say. I will paint to him the misery that must follow this accursed marriage, and if his heart is not turned to stone, he will break off the affair, and send Lord Danebury to look elsewhere for a bride."

"It must not be," cried Laura; "my father's welfare depends upon my yielding this point to him, and bitter indeed would be my after reflections should I see him suffering through any waywardness of my own."

"Then you can forget the friendship—love I had almost called it, that existed between us before the arrival of this hated lord?"

"It is unkind of you to remind me of this when I have no longer the power to help myself," cried Laura. "It is a duty to yield ourselves to circumstances, however painful it may be to us, and though I cannot regard you as I once did, I can still love you as a brother. Let us, I beseech you, forget the past, and it will avoid many a pang that must otherwise afflict us."

"How can I forget the past," exclaimed Stephen, "when I know that my much loved prize is in the possession of a rival?"

"You may not forget it," she replied, "but it is possible so to curb your passions that I may henceforth become an object of indifference to you."

"Never!" he exclaimed; "the moment that sees you the wife of Lord Danebury seals my unhappiness for ever."

"Nay, this is a weakness that you will soon learn to conquer," replied Miss Campbell. "The chief pang is sustained at first, but time is the great restorative, and, ere long, you will cease to feel the great regard for me that you do now. Let it ever be in your remembrance that I only act the part of a dutiful child who sees no other alternative to relieve her father from the consequence of his indiscretions."

"Yet a word of explanation to him," replied Stephen, "would save you from the consequences of this ill-assorted marriage."

"And that word must never be spoken," she exclaimed. "I might avoid a union with Lord Danebury, but could I ever be happy, think you, if I saw my father suffering because I would not make a sacrifice in his behalf? No, no, Stephen, my destiny in fixed—I become the wife of this man whom I can never love, but there will at least be the satisfaction of knowing that I have performed a sacred duty to my father."

Florence entered the room at this moment, and as she was followed almost immediately afterwards by Lord Danebury and Major Campbell, Stephen took his leave to return home. The conversation he had had with Laura was the sole subject of his thought, and heavy enough he found it when he was compelled to confess to himself that all hope of obtaining the hand of Miss Campbell was at an end. At length he reached the garden belonging to the Manor-house, where he found Mr. Beaumont, who, perceiving his dejection, inquired the reason of it.

" I have been to Major Campbell, sir," he replied, " and find that there is no exaggeration in the report that Laura is about to become the wife of this newly-arrived nobleman."

" And what is that to us, Stephen?" demanded the old gentleman ; " unless, indeed, you have been foolish enough to neglect my advice by running headlong into love with the girl yourself."

" It would be vain to deny it," answered Stephen. " I loved Miss Campbell, and believed that no obstacle stood in the way of my happiness till this Lord Danebury made his appearance."

" And now you suffer for not taking my advice," exclaimed Mr. Beaumont. " You are rightly served, Stephen, and——but hang it, I won't make you more miserable than you already seem to be, so let us change the subject. Did you happen to see this Lord Danebury in the course of your visit to the Clock-house?"

" I did."

" Was your name mentioned before him?"

" It was, sir."

" Did he make any remark, or exhibit any perturbation at discovering who you were ?"

" I fancied he was slightly startled at first," replied Stephen, " but that quickly disappeared, and then he affected great friendship towards me, and offered to provide me with a situation under government if I thought proper to accept it."

" Accept no favour from him, Stephen, unless you would bring down upon yourself my heaviest maledictions ! He is a villain, and when least he expects it I will drag him forth to the scorn and execration of the world."

" You have known each other previously ?" said the young man ; " indeed, he acknowledged as much to me himself."

" In early life we were acquainted, as I have already told you," replied Mr. Beaumont, " and circumstances that then passed between us can never be forgotten. I have called him a villain, and can prove my words should it be necessary."

" And this is the man," cried Stephen, " who is to become the husband of Laura Campbell !"

" He thinks himself secure of his prize," exclaimed the old man ; " but he shall be disappointed in a manner that he least expects. I have my eye on him, and hating him as I do he shall not escape me when the proper moment arrives. So, make yourself easy on that point, for my word is given, and I never break t, that he shall not marry the daughter of Major Campbell."

He turned abruptly away as if with a wish of avoiding further conversation, and Stephen Harland was once more left to the free indulgence of his own meditations.

CHAPTER XII.

Is thy love sincere? if 'tis indeed so
Thou wilt forsake thy home—nay, e'en thy friends,
To follow me in exi'e.—*Old Play.*

IT was at about this period that as Edward Cavendish was one day in the direction of the Clock House, he was overtaken by a violent tempest, and as no other shelter was at hand he hurried towards a ruined fishing temple that stood upon the estate of Major Campbell, but which had long since been disused in consequence of the dilapidation into which it had fallen. As he approached he saw that the door stood ajar, but when he had reached it within a few paces it was slammed to with violence, and then the creaking of rusty bolts within was distinctly audible.

Thinking it was one of the major's servants who had been out to look after the place, he knocked loudly, and demanded admittance, but his appeal was unheeded —no voice responded to him, and the only sound to be heard was the echo which he had roused by his own clatter against the door. This struck him as being singular, but as there was a mystery in it he resolved to clear it up, and remembering that there was a window with a balcony overhanging the water, and making his way round the building, he, with no little difficulty, succeeded in climbing up, and to his gratification he found that the window had been left unfastened. As quietly as possible he stepped in, and crossing the floor on tip-toe, was making his way towards an adjoining room, when the sound of persons whispering together struck upon his ear, and as he was going to call to them he heard the rough tones of a man exclaim :—

" It seems then that all I have been saying is in vain ; you are afraid of your father's anger, and prefer remaining with him to following the man that you have professed to love."

" These reproaches are most unkind," replied a female, whom Edward recognized to be Florence Campbell ; ",you know what risks I have run in your behalf, and that I would willingly encounter others to ensure your safety, yet nothing can satisfy you unless I leave my father's house to follow the uncertain fortunes of a fugitive."

" And why should you not do so ?" he inquired ; " do I not love you as well as your father, and have I not your promise that you will marry no one but me, let who will oppose it ?"

" True," she sighed ; " but this is no time to talk of love ; men are in pursuit of you in every direction. They are still certain that you have not left the neighbourhood, and it is only by remaining yet longer in this place of concealment that you can hope to escape their vigilance."

" It's all very well to talk about staying in this dungeon of a place," replied the other, " but a fellow that has always been used to his liberty would sooner die than be cooped up as I am."

" Ah, Paul !" she exclaimed ; " but what a death would yours be should you happen to fall into the hands of these men. I have heard it whispered that many a man has been hanged for a crime of less importance than the one you have committed, and, oh, think, I beseech you, what would be my agony should an ignominious fate be yours."

" But I have lived some time past in the expectation that such would be my end," he replied ; " and if it is so, there can be no help for it. I'm not afraid of dying, my girl, though, for your sake, I should like, if possible, to get out of this scrape."

" And so you may," replied Florence, " if you will only be guided by me. Remain here a few days more, and when the search begins to cool a little you can make your escape to another country till it is safe to return back to England."

" I'll not stir unless you go with me."

" It is impossible," she exclaimed ; " my father's curse would be upon me should I leave his house to follow the man whom he has forbidden me ever to see again. If you really love me, Paul, you will urge me no further on this subject."

" Do you doubt my truth, then ?" he demanded, sullenly.

" Heaven is my witness that I do not," she replied. " You have seen me forget the duty I owe to my father to give you these stolen meetings. I have risked the world's censure should these private assignations become known ;— yet all have been dared rather than you should have cause to believe that my heart has grown cold amidst the troubles that have befallen you."

" Well, don't tell me of the obligations I am under to you," exclaimed Paul ; " I know you to be a good, faithful creature to me, Florence, yet methinks you might prove your affection by following me, since it is likely I may never return again."

"You ask more than I can accede to," answered Florence. "My father, whatever other faults he may have, has ever proved most indulgent to his children, and it would be a base act of ingratitude to bring sorrow upon him in his last few years."

"In other words, you will not marry me without his consent?"

"Such," she replied, "is my present determination."

"Then, of course, I may make up my mind to consider the affair between us at an end?"

"Nay," she cried, earnestly, "I see no reason for believing that delay can lead to such a termination. My father has once held you high in his regard, and will do so again, if you prove yourself worthy of it."

"How is it to be done?"

"By renouncing your evil ways," she replied. "Become once again what you were before the accursed infatuation of gaming took possession of your soul; prove to him that you are not a slave to vice, and you shall not want my aid towards procuring a reconciliation."

"By my soul, girl," exclaimed Paul, "one would imagine by your words that Major Campbell is so free from vice that he cannot endure to see it in others."

"Far be it from me to speak of my father's weakness," she replied; "I know that he has been addicted to the accursed crime of gaming, but I also hope that he has at last awakened to a sense of shame that will lead to his entire reformation."

"Ay," answered the other, "now that he has squandered away all that he possessed he will abjure a course of life that he can no longer pursue. The truth is, Florence, those who were ready enough to fleece him when he had money, now turn their backs upon him, since it is known that he has not a feather left to fly with. Such is the world's way, my girl; and I have always foreseen that your father would go on, in the hope of retrieving his fortune, till he became the victim of a set of merciless sharpers."

"You think, then, he is ruined?" cried Florence, in accents of despair.

"I am sure of it," answered Paul; "nay, more, he has had several large advances from your sister, which he will never be able to repay, and hence arises his anxiety to marry his elder daughter to this nobleman. Lord Danebury knows all the circumstances, because he has had a principal hand in robbing your father of his money, and now he would wed the daughter, because he knows she has still a very large fortune at her own disposal."

"Alas!" she sighed, "then the destiny of my sister is even worse than I imagined."

"She is doomed to misery if she weds this heartless old lord," answered Paul. "I have long had my eye on him, and know more of his villany than he has any idea of. Perhaps, if it is not too late, you may devise some scheme for preventing a marriage that threatens such evil consequences."

"I am afraid that will be impossible," said Florence; "for, though my sister loves not this Lord Danebury, she consents to receive his addresses in consequence of the express commands of her father. Inclination is sacrificed to duty, and much do I fear that all will terminate in suffering and despair."

"At any rate," answered Paul, "you can warn her against giving any further encouragement to his lordship."

"The task would be a vain one," replied Florence; "for she already regards him with dislike, yet has resolved to accompany him to the altar in deference to her father's wish."

"Even as you refuse to become mine for the same reason," exclaimed the other.

"You wrong me, Paul," she replied; "have I not promised to reject all other offers for your sake, and can you believe that I will forfeit my word, even should your absence be longer than we expect?"

" I know women are fickle, and 'out of sight out of mind' is an old saying that I have often observed is a very true one. When I am gone some one else takes my place, and I shall be left to reconcile myself to my cruel fate in the best way I may."

" Can you believe this of me, Paul?" she cried. " You say women are fickle—but in love, where will you find such enduring constancy as in our sex?"

" Let those place their faith in it who have more confidence than I pretend to," answered Paul. " In short, Florence, you must fly with me this very night, if you would prove your love."

" I cannot—dare not."

" Ha! do you refuse?"

" How—how can I do otherwise?"

" I ask you not how it is to be done," he replied, " for the desperation of the moment leaves me no other alternative than the one I have mentioned. If I am truly loved, you will not hesitate to leave father, sister, home, all—all for me. In another land we may find safety and happiness,—here, I am in hourly dread of shame and degradation."

" Then escape whilst you have the power to do so," she exclaimed, entreatingly.

" Never!" exclaimed Paul; " you have convinced me that your love is no longer mine, and now I care not what fate destiny has in store for me. Let them send me to the gibbet, and I can die resigned, since your scorn has made life utterly worthless."

" Your words terrify me," cried Florence; " tell me, Paul Rayland, what dreadful threat do these words of yours imply?"

" That I will surrender myself this very hour to those who are searching for me."

" No, no, no!" she wildly cried; " you surely cannot meditate such an act of madness?"

" A very short time will prove to you whether I do or not," he replied. " Why should I wish to avoid my fate any longer? Would you have me wander alone on the face of the earth, without one to console me for the past, or a friend to inspire my bosom with hope for the future?"

" And could I do aught to soften the cruel harshness of your exile?"

" Ay," he replied; " your society would be all that I desire, let my wanderings lead me where they may. I am of a wild and wayward disposition, Florence, but kindness never yet failed to reach my heart, and I believe your gentle counsel might yet work the best effects upon me. Say, then, will you consent to leave home with me this night, or shall I surrender myself at once to justice?"

" I—I—will go with you," said Florence, in a tone that was scarcely audible.

" But will you do so willingly," he asked, " or must I afterwards endure reproaches for having been the cause of your leaving home?"

" Believe me, Paul, I will never utter a complaint," she replied. " It is for the sake of your happiness that I take this step, and, let my sufferings and privations be what they may, I will endure all with patience, so that I can but see your love as lasting as my own shall be."

" It is agreed, then, that we leave this place together, Florence?"

" It is."

" To-night?"

" Ay, if it is your will."

" Then at the hour of twelve, the gipsy woman, whom you have before seen, shall be at the gate of your father's mansion. She is faithful, and, I believe, may be relied on. Follow her without dread, and she will lead you to the place where I shall be waiting to receive you."

" I will not fail," replied Florence, " to leave the house at the time you have named. The step is one upon which misery or happiness may depend, and, oh! may I never have reason to repent the hour when I forsook the home of my birth to become the companion of one whom I have loved well, but I fear not wisely."

"Do you begin to repine already?" demanded Paul.

"No," she replied; "but it is impossible to avoid these thoughts at such a moment as this. But 'tis now past—all shall yield to the one consideration, that my word has been solemnly pledged, and it shall be kept, though misery and hopeless wandering should be the consequence."

"It is enough," exclaimed Paul, "I will rely upon your promise; and at the hour of midnight we shall meet again—farewell! be punctual, or the next you hear of Paul Rayland will be, that he is an inmate of your county gaol."

He turned from her, and was about to leave the room, when Edward Cavendish, springing forward with a loud cry of vengeance, seized him by the throat with so strong a grasp that the fugitive found it impossible, notwithstanding his superior strength, to release himself. A violent struggle then ensued between them, while Florence stood by, fixed and motionless as a statue; she had no power to aid her lover, who each moment grew more helpless in the grasp of his adversary; but at length, as he fell beneath Cavendish, she rushed forward, and in the most piteous accents of supplication, emplored mercy for the fallen man.

"He deserves none!" exclaimed Edward, still retaining his hold, "nor shall he have any from me, unless he promises to renounce all further pretensions to your hand."

"Fool!" muttered Paul; "think you I am to be vanquished by a man that I have ever held in my contempt! For a moment only you have obtained the mastery over me; presently we shall be on a more equal footing, and it shall then be seen who it is that has to make terms with the other. Take your hands from me, presumptuous boy, or this place shall be your tomb."

"I am not to be intimidated from my purpose," answered Edward. "Fortune has sent me hither to thwart your schemes against this too confiding girl, and never will I yield up my present advantage till you have solemnly promised to urge her no more to quit her father's house."

"Why do you trouble yourself with an affair that concerns you not?" demanded the fugitive. "The girl has a right to give her heart to whom she pleases, and why not to me as well as any one else?"

"Because I know you for a villain, who would remorselessly destroy her happiness. She has weakly listened to your protestations of love, and has believed them, though they are as false as your own heart."

"I wooed her honourably," replied Paul, gradually becoming less violent. "The girl has had opportunity enough to judge whether I am the villain you represent me, and as she is satisfied with my honourable intentions, you might have spared yourself the trouble of interfering where you were not needed."

"Had your intentions been as honourable as you profess," exclaimed Edward Cavendish, "it would have been your first care to see her father upon the subject, and ascertain the views he has taken with respect to the proposed union. Instead of that, however, you woo her in secret—induce her to leave home, when all are locked in the arms of sleep, and at length, when the place is too hot to hold you any longer, you persuade her to fly from the protection of a parent to become the companion of a fugitive."

"All that may be very true, and yet no great harm done either," exclaimed Paul. "I did persuade her to go with me, but is that to be wondered at when I found I could never be happy without her? and as for asking her father's consent, it was out of the question, as he, like yourself, has formed a most unfortunate prejudice against me."

"Release him, Edward Cavendish, I implore you!" cried Florence, who by this time had, in some degree, recovered from her agitation. "If there is blame in this affair, let it fall upon me, for I alone am guilty; since he would have left the place long ago but for the encouragement I afforded him."

"And did you know," demanded Edward, "that your lover was no other than the notorious fugitive, Paul Rayland, for whose apprehension a large reward has been offered?"

"I cannot plead ignorance as an excuse," she replied; "I knew who and what he was, yet such was the strength of my attachment that I could not tear him from my heart as you would have me do."

"Now, Edward Cavendish, do you blame me for trying to prevail on her to flee with me?" asked the fugitive. "She acknowledges her love, and I now ask you if I should not have been less than man had I refused to accept a heart that I well knew was all my own. So now release me, for my rage has grown cooler, and I pledge my word that this contest between us shall not be renewed by me."

Edward Cavendish relaxed his hold, and, as the other instantly sprang upon his feet, he exclaimed, addressing himself to Florence,—

"You have heard the opinion this young gentleman has thought proper to express of me, and perhaps his words have not been without their effect upon you; say, then, am I to expect you to-night according to our former agreement?"

"It shall be my task to prevent it," replied Edward; "for I shall keep watch on the house of Major Campbell, and should his daughter attempt to leave it, I shall alarm the inmates. I have no wish thus far to expose her to the evil remarks of the world, and she will therefore do well to fail in her appointment, as, in that case, it will not be necessary for me to say a word about what has transpired here to-day."

"Well," exclaimed Paul, "you have contrived to get the best of me for once, and I suppose I must submit for the present. But you have heard the girl acknowledge that she loves me, and nothing shall prevent her being mine as soon as I can find a place to take her to. So here we part, Edward Cavendish, luckily for you with whole bones; but remember, I may not be so easily overcome another time, and I would therefore advise you to keep clear of me, or I may serve you worse than I did Stephen Harland the last time we saw each other."

With a haughty inclination of the head to Florence, and a look of scornful defiance at Edward, the fugitive moved slowly away, left the ruined building, and, crossing an intervening road was soon lost to the view of those who stood gazing after him. Cavendish then offered to accompany Florence towards her home, which, with some little reluctance, she acceded to, and as they proceeded on their way, Edward ventured to inquire if the meeting of which he had been a witness had occurred by accident.

"It was not," she replied; "I knew where he was, and, leaving home by stealth, went to see if I could prevail on him to escape from England while there was yet a chance of doing so."

"Has he been secreted in the ruin long?" inquired Edward Cavendish.

"Nearly a week," she replied.

"And being aware of it," exclaimed the other, "you gave no intimation to the persons who have been so long in search of him?"

"I would have perished first!" cried Florence; "it was I who counselled him to seek shelter in the place where you just saw him, and base indeed should I have been to set his foes on him."

"I am only surprised," observed the young man, "that no one ever thought of searching the place."

"Who would have expected to find him in any part of my father's premises?" demanded Florence. "I cautioned him never to be seen at the door or window, and whenever an opportunity favoured me, I visited him to convey such provisions as he needed."

"And all this," exclaimed Edward, "has been done to save from a deserved fate the villain who would have murdered Stephen Harland!"

"That he did not accomplish so dreadful an end, we have all of us reason to be thankful," replied the maiden. "Happily Stephen has escaped, and I trust he will have too much magnanimity to seek for revenge against an unfortunate fellow-being who already has too many enemies to contend against."

"He is too dangerous a man to be at liberty," replied Edward Cavendish. "We have had sufficient proof of his reckless disposition, and though once foiled in his attempt on the life of my friend, he may not miss his object the next time he comes across him."

"Take my word for it, Stephen has nothing more to fear from him," exclaimed Florence Campbell. "There was, I believe, no premeditation when the rencontre took place between them, and had the death of your friend ensued, no one would have regretted it more than he who is now hunted for through the country like a wild beast."

"I believe Paul felt some jealousy when he saw Harland walking towards your father's house," observed the other. "He suspected, perhaps, that the visit was intended for you, and hence arose the quarrel that had nearly terminated fatally."

"Such may have been the fact," answered Florence; "but I have always avoided asking Paul any questions about it, because I could see that he would rather avoid the subject. But see, I am now nearly at home, and lest any inquiries should be made, I must request you to permit me to go the remainder of the way alone."

Edward Cavendish acceded to her suggestion, and as he once more cautioned her against giving Paul Rayland any further meetings, she bounded away, as if unwilling to hear a word against the fugitive.

CHAPTER XIII.

Hear me, my child—canst thou unmoved behold
The ruin of thy father ? Thou hast heard
How sure destruction follows thy refusal;
That beggary's my lot—yet still thy tongne
Is mute.   Thou wilt refuse me !—*The Forced Marriage.*

EACH succeeding day Laura, with increasing alarm, saw that her destiny was fixed, and that nothing short of her union with Lord Danebury would save her misguided father from the poverty that his unfortunate love of gaming threatened him with. He now more frequently urged her to give a decided answer to her noble wooer ; but hitherto she had been able, under various excuses, to gain more time ere she pronounced the fatal words that she felt assured would plunge her into a life of unhappiness.

Hitherto Lord Danebury had not pressed his suit with the ardour that might have been expected from him ; yet this was from no considerate feelings, but rather that he knew the prize was safe whenever he thought proper to demand it, and he could therefore assume an appearance of delicacy in his attentions, that at any other time, or with any other person, he would not have had the magnanimity to display. Major Campbell affected to be enraptured with this proof of his lordship's excellence of heart, and he failed not to direct his daughter's attention to it ; but Laura was not to be so easily deceived by mere outward show, for she had formed a tolerably just estimate of the nobleman's character, and her dislike for him increased as she saw that to his other deformities of mind he added that of the deepest dissimulation.   Her father became more and more impatient as she still manifested a disinclination to speak her mind freely to him on the subject, and one evening, after he had been drinking pretty freely with his guest, he abruptly entered the room where his daughter was at work, and throwing himself into a chair by her side, he exclaimed, with more than customary excitement,—

" I am come, Laura, to see if we cannot bring matters to bear a little better than they do at present.   Lord Danebury has been our guest for some days past ; you are aware of the motive that has caused the honour of a visit, yet nothing decisive has yet been uttered upon the subject.   Tell me, then, in one word, whether I am to expect your ready submission to the wish I have already on so many occasions expressed."

" And I have told you," answered Laura, " that the subject is too weighty a one to be decided on without long and careful consideration."

" What consideration can it possibly require ?" demanded Major Campbell. " Here is a chance that any other girl would have jumped at without giving it a second thought, yet you must needs require days ere you can make up your mind to share a coronet with a man who ranks amongst the proudest in the English peerage."

" A coronet possesses no attractions for me," replied Laura, " unless I am first assured that the wearer of it has never done anything to disgrace the high position he is placed in."

" And who, pray, has put this romantic stuff into your head?" asked her father, impatiently.

" I speak my own thoughts, sir," she replied, " and grieved shall I be if you are offended with me for exercising the prudence you have ever taught me was necessary, ere a female contracted an alliance that is not made for a day, a week, or a year, but for the whole term of existence."

" That is all very good," replied the major, " and I am glad to find my lessons in prudence have not been thrown away.   But there can be no objection raised against Lord Danebury ; in wealth and station he is surpassed by none."

" So I have heard before," answered Laura ; " but all the wealth he possesses will not purchase me one hour's happiness, if he is really what the world says of him."

" The world !" exclaimed her father ; " and pray, what does the world say of him ?"

" That he is a gambler, who has increased his own wealth at the expence of those whom he has found means to inveigle into his snares."

" They wrong him, then, most foully," cried the major, warmly. " I will admit he plays a good deal, but whatever gains he makes are fairly won. I have been often with him on such occasions, and can declare that he never takes an advantage such as I have seen others do."

" Perhaps he is more cautious," observed Laura, " and thus avoids detection where others have not the skill to hide their villany."

" You are too severe."

" I hope it may be so ; but, as a professed gambler, I can only regard him with aversion."

" And that aversion will be my ruin," exclaimed Major Campbell, with agitation. " I am indebted to his lordship some thousands of pounds ; all of which he is willing to cancel on one condition."

" Which is, that I become his wife !"

" Exactly."

" Have you considered the sacrifice ?"

" I can see none," answered her father ; " the marriage is in every way a most desirable one, and yet you would blindly throw away a chance such as you never had any reason to expect."

" I neither expected nor desired it," answered Laura ; " my ambition was never so soaring, and should I ever marry at all, I should prefer uniting my destiny with some estimable man whose rank in life was not superior to my own."

" Why, this is the motive of a foolish girl who has gleaned all her experience from love-books and romances."

" Nay, that can hardly be, for I never read them."

" Then you have some foolish friends, whose advice I counsel you henceforward to avoid. Your father's commands should be superior to all else, and if you think proper to disobey them, it will be at your own peril."

" You are angry with me, sir."

" I shall be so presently," replied the major, " unless some hope is held out that you are likely to become a little more reasonable. However, his lordship, I believe, intends to request an interview with you upon the subject, and it is my most earnest request, Laura, that you do not offend him by a direct refusal. Ask for time to consider the matter, if you please, but crush not his hopes at a single blow, or I know not how soon I may be made to feel for the obstinacy of my child."

" Think you," cried Laura, " his vengeance would fall upon one, who is not to blame in the affair ?"

" I am certain of it."

" Then people must have spoken truly of him," replied his daughter " and the dislike I felt before is increased by your avowal."

" What avowal ?"

" That he is revengeful, and would hurl his fury upon those who have not the power to resist him."

" Nay, I said not that he would seek to bring about my ruin, but that he might do so if provoked by obstinacy of yours."

" But I have reason to believe that such is his real character," answered Laura. " Indeed, indeed, my dear father, I cannot make up my mind to give away my hand without my heart. It would be committing perjury at the altar were I to do so, and my soul revolts from uttering words of falsehood in the face of heaven."

" You refuse, then, to accept this offer, by which alone I can be saved from ruin ?"

" I must think further of it," she replied ; " command me to do aught else, and even were it to walk barefoot through the world, I would do so rather than unite myself to a man who loves me not."

" This is mighty well !" ejaculated the major, through his firmly clenched teeth. " A father has humbled himself to ask a favour from his child, and has been refused.

But hear me, girl—I am no longer to be trifled with.   Obey my commands, and we are friends— disobey them, and I cast you for ever from my heart as a serpent that I have nurtured only to perish by its sting at last."

"Oh ! why do you thus urge me," she wildly cried, "when I have said, that as the wife of Lord Danebury, I must be wedded to misery ?   I have seen enough of him to know that he is cold of heart, and only professes love for me in furtherance of certain schemes that he has yet to put in practice against you."

"This is nothing but a groundless suspicion," exclaimed Major Campbell, "and was least expected from you, who, I have always thought, gave no expression to opinions that could not be well substantiated.   You speak of Lord Danebury with disgust ; but, in the first place, what have you to say to his figure ?"

"That it is almost as deformed as his mind."

"His age ?"

"Would render him more fit to be my grandfather than my husband."

"His fortune ?"

"Is said to be large ; but what is that, if the possessor is worthless ?"

"You are too severe, Laura," exclaimed her father.   "His lordship has some very excellent qualities, amongst which I will name his generosity.   He aspires to no more riches than he at present possesses, and would marry you, even if I gave you to him portionless."

"So you imagine," replied Laura ; "but such is not my own opinion of him. He knows that I possess a fortune, or Lord Danebury would never have thought of me for a wife."

"Hush !—I think I hear his footstep coming this way," whispered the major. "If it should be so, receive him with gentleness and courtesy, for if it must be that this match is broken off, I would defer the explanation as long as possible."

"Oh, do not let me see him !" cried Laura, in accents of terror ; "spare me, I entreat, from an interview at this moment, for I feel that I should expire at his feet."

"Calm your apprehensions, foolish girl," said her father ; "for it seems I was mistaken ; his lordship is not coming, as I imagined, so you will have time to recover yourself ere the interview that you seem to anticipate with so much dread.   So now tell me, is there no hope that, upon reflection, you may think better of this ?"

"It is impossible."

"And why impossible ?"

"Your question," cried Laura, "will draw from me a confession that I would not have made now.   I will not, however, deceive you, and therefore I at once acknowledge that my heart is already engaged to another."

"Ha ! and this has been kept a secret from me !"

"It has," sighed Laura ; "but only because I feared your displeasure."

"And pray," he asked, "who is the happy object of your romantic love ?"

"Stephen Harland."

"Indeed !" exclaimed the major ; "well, it must be confessed he is a likely young fellow enough, and, but for his lordship, I know not that I should have raised an objection to the match.   So let him dangle after you, my girl, for it would hardly be wise to dismiss him ; and then if, after all, you should persist in not becoming Lady Danebury, you can sink down quietly into plain Mistress Harland.   The youngster is a most excellent fellow, and I am not altogether sorry that he is not so blind as to pass over the perfections of my daughter."

"You will have no objection to him, then, in case he should speak to you on the subject ?"

"Perhaps not ; but he must not ask me yet, though," replied her father.   "We must not let his lordship know just yet that he is to be rejected, or I shall not be prepared for the course I have every reason to believe he will adopt."

"Have you any fresh pecuniary engagements to him then ?" asked Laura, with alarm.

"Ay, and very heavy ones, my love," he replied.   "It must be confessed that I am deeply involved, and once more I shall be forced to ask you to extricate me from my difficulties.   I have property to sell, but it must not be disposed of to a disadvantage, and when the sale has been completed, I will repay you all that has been advanced."

"I can refuse you nothing, except to become the wife of Lord Danebury," cried Laura. "What money I have is freely at your disposal; relieve yourself from these dreadful embarrassments—dismiss his lordship from our presence, and I shall be happy, even though beggary may be my portion."

"Nay, there is nothing so bad as that to be feared," answered her father. "A few thousands will serve to set me right with the world, and then I can snap my fingers at his lordship, however angry he may be at your rejection of him. Forgive me for being angry with you just now, but ruin stared me in the face, and I knew not what I said. But the money you have placed at my disposal sets matters square again, and we will have no more words, so that you will but be tolerably civil to his lordship till I am out of his power."

He left the room with more cheerfulness than he had exhibited for some days past, and upon being left to herself, Laura Campbell gave way to the various and conflicting thoughts that the recent conversation had engendered in her mind. Her father's avowed difficulties were her chief source of uneasiness; for he had long since squandered away nearly the whole of his patrimony, and the frequent demands that he had recently made upon her fortune gave rise to serious apprehensions that poverty would overtake them all, unless he could be prevailed upon to relinquish his visits to the gaming-table. The only hope that remained was in her own influence over him, and relying in a great measure upon this, she was about to leave the room in search of her sister, when Stephen Harland unexpectedly presented himself before her. A smile of joy instantly overspread her countenance, and, with a gaiety that she had not recently exhibited, she said,—

"This visit is indeed most welcome to me; I have been thinking of you, but perhaps if I were to say how much, you would grow so vain that there would be no bearing with you afterwards."

"May I inquire," he asked, with a smile, "the nature of your thoughts?"

"Only as far as I think proper to tell you," she replied. "In truth, Stephen, I have had rather an unpleasant interview with my father just now, and he has insisted that I shall receive Lord Danebury as my accepted lover."

"And you have ——"

"Refused to do anything of the kind," she replied, interrupting; "I have spoken my mind more freely than I ever did before, and we nearly got into a terrible quarrel that might have ended in my being discarded for ever from his house."

"I can guess it all," sighed the young man; "you at length yielded to your father's threats, and it is my hard destiny to lose a prize which I value far more highly than life itself."

"Nay," answered Laura, "I believe affairs will turn out better than I expected. My father began to relent when he saw that I was not to be won by the title he proposed for me, and the matter ended with a promise, on my part, to treat his lordship with civility, and to defer my rejection of his suit till arrangements have been made for the settlement of certain large debts of honour that are due to Lord Danebury."

"And the necessary sum must, of course, be provided by you?"

"'Tis even so," she replied. "My father's blindness hurries him more and more towards ruin, and though he is hourly cheated by those who prey upon him, he attributes all his losses to bad luck. Thus he is tempted to try again—the same thing occurs, and so it will, I am afraid, till he has brought irretrievable ruin upon himself."

"'Tis fearful to think of!" exclaimed Stephen Harland; "and I believe the principal portion of the money he is cheated out of finds its way into the pocket of this honourable lord."

"It does."

"Yet this is the man your father is so anxious for you to marry?"

"Yes, Stephen; and nothing that anybody can say to him will ever induce a belief but what everything is conducted with the most perfect honesty and fairness."

"Would that it were in my power," he exclaimed, "to offer myself to your father as a suitor for the hand of his daughter. But, unfortunately, I am poor—without a home to call my own, and almost friendless. Thus situated, how can I venture to allow myself one solitary gleam of hope that my humble pretensions would be listened to?"

"Your fate is only involved in mystery for the present," answered Laura; "and who knows but an unexpected turn of good fortune may yet reward you. With my father you are an exceeding great favourite, and if this Lord Danebury were but once fairly dismissed, I know not but he would as soon accept you for a son-in-law as anybody else."

"Has he ever spoken of me?"

"Ay, within the last half hour."

"And with favour?"

"Yes; he said he had a very great regard for you," replied Laura. "But regard stands for naught when interest is in the way; and, as he has been dazzled with a title, I suppose he will not give up the notion of my being the wife of a peer till his lordship grows tired of this unprofitable wooing and goes elsewhere in search of a wife."

"You speak as lightly of this affair," said Stephen, "as if the happiness of two persons were not in the scale."

"That is because I begin to discover that sorrow does not remove the cause of our uneasiness," replied Laura. "I was at first dull enough, as you know, but now I mean to try what a little good-humoured gaiety will do. His lordship, I hear, has a terrible aversion to what he calls forward women, and perhaps I may frighten him away when he discovers that I am not the prudish, stiff, starch body that he took me for."

"His wife you may never be," exclaimed Stephen; "but that will hardly mend my situation, since there is scarcely a chance that Major Campbell will consent to my marriage with his daughter."

"That remains to be proved," she replied, "and, as I am to have some voice in it, your condition may not be quite so desperate as you imagine. You must, however, absent yourself from the house for some days to come, for Lord Danebury has been jealous ever since he saw you here the other day, and perhaps he might be induced to stay longer should he meet you here again, if it should only be for the sake of drawing you into a quarrel that might end in a duel."

"He would find that I should not hesitate to meet him even in such an instance as that," exclaimed Stephen Harland.

"Nay," she cried, "that must never be permitted. Lord Danebury is reported to be an accomplished swordsman, and a duel with such a man is almost like rushing blindly into the arms of death. Keep therefore away from our house for the present, and when he is gone you can continue to pay your visits here with the same freedom as formerly."

"But shall I be a welcome guest to your father?"

"My father, I repeat, entertains a very great regard for you," answered Laura; "more, I may say, than I ever saw him exhibit towards anybody else excepting his own daughters. He will always give you a welcome, Stephen, and, in time, it is not at all unlikely that he will permit you to pay your addresses to me as some recompense for the loss of his more exalted son-in-law."

"Are you serious, dear Laura?"

"I have had little reason to be otherwise of late," she replied, "for I have been obliged to make myself a prisoner in my own room, in order to avoid meeting with his lordship, whose affected civilities I am scarcely able to endure. In truth, I would almost as soon become the wife of Paul Rayland, as of this antiquated peer, who, I verily believe, has been the cause of my father's more frequent attendance at the gaming-table."

"Talking of Paul Rayland," said Stephen, "there is a report that he has contrived to escape, after being concealed in the neighbourhood for several days."

"So much the better," said Laura; "for, bad as he is, I should have been sorry if they had caught him, since his attack upon your life might have led to the forfeiture of his own."

"Have you no other reason for being glad that he has escaped?" asked the young man.

"I know to what you allude when you put that question," answered Laura. "You have heard, of course, that my sister Florence has formed an unfortunate attachment for him, which even his crimes have failed to remove."

"But," said Stephen Harland, "they were upon friendly terms, I believe, before he became the reckless fellow that he has since proved?"

"They were regarded as lovers," answered Laura; "though even at that time Paul was anything but what we could have wished him. He was one of the frequenters of the same gaming-house to which my father and Lord Danebury resorted, and when at length he became utterly ruined, he associated himself with the most abandoned and depraved of mankind, till you see him reduced to his present miserable condition. But let us speak no more of him, for my heart grows sick whenever I recollect the unfortunate attachment my sister has formed for him. I expect a visit presently from Lord Danebury, and as the rencontre between you might not be a very pleasant one, I must be so far inhospitable as to request you to leave me till you can visit us with greater freedom."

"Since it is your wish, I will take my leave," said Stephen Harland, "but it is from no disinclination to meet Lord Danebury, who I hold so much beneath my contempt, that scarcely anything he might say would draw forth a word of resentment."

"It will be better to avoid all chance of a quarrel," said Laura, "and therefore I again request as a favour that you will not meet him at present. Leave me, Stephen; and perhaps ere long I shall have an opportunity of declaring to his lordship the utter uselessness of his wasting time in this ill-advised project of his. Then, if my father consents, there will be no further occasion for an interruption in your visits to our house."

Stephen Harland was not allowed to make any reply, for persons were heard approaching, and, disappointed by the interruption, he bade a hasty adieu to Laura Campbell, and instantly quitted her presence.

CHAPTER XIV.

Loosed to the world's wide range, enjoined no aim,
Prescribed no duty, and assigned no name:
Nature's unbounded son, he stands alone,
His heart unbiass'd and his mind his own.—SAVAGE.

STEPHEN returned homeward with a heavy heart, for, in spite of all the assurances he had received from Laura, the position of affairs at the Clock-house were well calculated to raise doubts in his mind. His agitation was observed by Mr. Beaumont, who endeavoured to console him with hopes of better prospects.

In the course of conversation with the old gentleman, Stephen learned that the former had received a letter from Lord Danebury, offering to procure for the young man a situation, which would materially improve his prospects in life. This caused considerable surprise in the mind of Stephen, who knew of no reason why his lordship should be so pressing in bestowing a kindness upon him, the more especially as he had received all his overtures with such coolness.

Mr. Beaumont, after hinting that Lord Danebury might have found Stephen a dangerous rival, and in consequence wished to get him out of the way, confided to Stephen another reason, which perhaps might have induced the proffer of kindness— a reason, too, which raised in the young man's breast a thousand anxious feelings. He gave Stephen to understand, that though he had been treated as a son by old Mr. Hartland, it was to Lord Danebury he owed his existence, but that from his very birth he had not been indebted to him for a single kindness. Further than this, with the exception that he had not been born in wedlock, Mr. Beaumont refused to impart, and with what little knowledge he possessed, Stephen was obliged to be content, though he could not help some anxious fears arising in his breast, respecting the light in which Laura might regard his dishonourable birth.

As some slight set-off against the far from pleasing secret entrusted to him by Mr. Beaumont, that worthy man intimated to him that in consequence of Laura's coolness towards Lord Danebury, that nobleman had given orders for his immediate departure from the Clock-house ; and the old gentleman advised Stephen that he should at once endeavour to persuade Laura to consent to an early marriage, and thereby save the remains of her fortune, a greater part of which had been already dissipated by her dissolute father.

After giving this advice, Mr. Beaumont left Stephen to ruminate at leisure upon the subject, and to come to a conclusion as to what course he should pursue.

We will now return to Paul Rayland, who, after his escape, had again sought concealment in the Haunted Hollow. Night had come on rapidly, and, with a beating heart, the fugitive listened to the many sounds caused by the wind as it swept through the old ruins. Suddenly the echo of footsteps struck upon his ear, and then as suddenly died away in the distance.

While Paul was reflecting, with some degree of alarm, upon this circumstance, a light appeared at a slight distance, and in a few moments Rough Rob, his gipsy confederate, stood before him.

" Did you reach the ruins alone ?" asked Paul, anxiously.

" I did," was the reply ; " why do you ask ?"

Paul mentioned the footsteps he had heard, but Rob swore that it must have been caused solely by the owls and the bats.

With this explanation Paul was obliged to be satisfied ; and then he proceeded to unfold to Rough Rob a plan he had concocted for robbing the house of the young heir, Edward Cavendish, who had just come of age.

" The Priory," urged Paul, " is well stocked with plate and money ; the interior of the house is easily gained, and the danger from detection is but small, as there are but few servants."

Rob demurred at first, but when Paul hinted to him that Patty, the dairymaid, whom he had a liking for, might be induced by his means to become his wife, the gipsy acceded at once, and the next night was fixed for the attempt.

" The booty once obtained," exclaimed Paul, " my next task—no difficult one either—will be to induce Florence Campbell to fly with me, and in a foreign land we will forget the dangers we have experienced in England."

At this moment, to their great surprise, the figure of a man stepped forth from a niche in the ruins, and, as the light of Rob's lantern flashed upon his features, they recognized Richard Elliott, the lover of the very Patty whom they had just been plotting against.

By the words he uttered, Paul and his companion felt convinced that he had overheard the whole of their conversation, and they now pretended to treat it as a joke, asserting that they had been aware the whole of the time that he had been eaves-dropping, and that they concocted the whole for the purpose of frightening him.

Elliot, however, was not to be convinced, and they suddenly left him, disappearing in the darkness without his being able to discern their features.

CHAPTER XV.

For never was the gentle breast
Insensible to human woes ;
Feeling, though firm, it melts distress'd,
For weaknesses it never knows.—WALPOLE.

AT an unusually early hour in the morning following the events last narrated, Major Campbell returned home from one of those fatal visits to London which had brought such ruin upon him. His countenance on this occasion was flushed, and his eyes bloodshot, and his whole appearance betokened unusual agitation.

Instantly summoning his daughter Laura, an interview of the most painful and exciting description took place, in which he stated that Lord Danebury, angered at Laura's refusal, had insisted upon his (Major Campbell) discharging

several large debts of honour which he had incurred to him. Driven to despair by his inability to do so, the major had again resorted to the gaming-table, and in a few hours he had lost to so large an amount that even the whole of his daughter's fortune would have been insufficient to have paid it.

Laura listened to this recital with a heart trembling with alarm. She saw that, unless she consented to make herself a beggar, her father must be consigned to a prison; but she at once, with a resolution that could only emanate from a heart noble as her own, determined that the sacrifice should be made, and that every farthing she possessed should be divided fairly among her father's creditors.

Major Campbell, alarmed at the consequences of such a sacrifice, and the fearful effects it must have upon his daughter's prospects in life, refused her proffer, and that, too, with a steadiness of resolve that convinced Laura that he was in earnest.

"There is one proposition I have to make, my own dear Laura," said the major, "which is a mere trifle in comparison with the one you are so anxious to confer."

"What is it?" she eagerly asked.

"Lend me a sum of money—the amount of which shall be afterwards named—and I may, perhaps, be able to relieve myself from the difficulties in which I am now involved."

"You would seek the gaming-table once more, father?"

The major did not answer, but, from his countenance, Laura saw at once that her conjecture was but too correct.

There was a silence of some few moments, and then Laura said,—

"Do as you think best, father; all I have in the world is at your service, to rescue you from your present painful position."

The major, man of the world as he was, could not speak his thanks, but, wringing his daughter's hand, he left the room, while Laura sank almost senseless on a sofa, and gave way to a flood of tears.

*   *   *   *   *   *   *   *

About an hour after darkness had set in, on the night appointed for the robbery at the Priory, two figures might have been observed conversing at a little distance from the gipsy rendezvous near the Haunted Hollow. These persons were old Janet and the confederate of Paul Rayland, Rough Rob.

The latter had imparted to Janet the excursion on which he and Paul were going that night, and the old woman, in a solemn manner, had warned him to beware of the young reprobate, for that when his own purpose was suited he would no longer care for his fate.

"Let me alone for that," returned the gipsy; "I have an old score to settle with Paul, and it shall be deeply, terribly paid. It is convenient to be friendly with him now, but let him beware, for the fate of poor Susan, whom I loved dearer than life itself, and whom he won from me, and then saw her sink into the grave with a cold eye, has not been forgotten by me. Oh! Paul, Paul, my revenge shall yet come—shall yet come."

The form of the weather-beaten man shook with emotion, and he hid his face in his hands.

At this moment a footstep was heard, and Paul appeared. The gipsy instantly shook off the feeling that oppressed him, and dismissing the old woman, the two men set off towards the Priory.

The lights were fast disappearing in the different rooms, and after watching for about an hour, they determined at length to make the attempt to enter the house. An entrance was speedily effected in the rear of the mansion, and the robbers made their way to the upper part of the house, securing anything worth their carrying away in their progress thither.

Their search as yet not proving satisfactory, it was resolved that Rob should search the upper part of the house, while Paul remained below to find the strong room.

While the latter was thus engaged, he was suddenly seized from behind, and turning, he found himself in the grasp of the butler. A struggle ensued, and they rolled on the floor together, the butler keeping his grasp upon Paul.

"Villain!" exclaimed the domestic; "who are you, and what purpose has brought you here?"

For a moment Paul hesitated, and then he said,—

"I happened to overhear some gipsies planning to rob the house, and followed them unseen. While they broke in, I stood a little way off to watch their movements, and when they entered the place, I still pursued their steps, and was just thinking to look for them up stairs when you rushed upon me, as if I had been one of the robbers."

Before the butler could reply, Rough Rob flew past them with the speed of lightning, and dropping some of the articles with which he had helped himself, he made his way towards the door by which they had effected an entrance, and quitted the house. Upon seeing the fugitive rush past, the butler relaxed the grasp with which he held Paul Rayland, and instantly set off in pursuit of the retreating robber.

At this moment a number of domestics appeared, and Paul, drawing a pistol from his vest, cleared a way before him, and escaped into a shrubbery, and made his escape.

But the artifice Paul had used when in the power of the butler had been overheard by Rob, and he swore the most terrible vengeance against Rayland when an opportunity should occur.

On the morning succeeding the robbery, while Paul was strolling within a short distance of the gipsy encampment, he was startled to hear a strange voice call him by name, and, on looking round to discover from whence it proceeded, he, to his great surprise, beheld the form of Edward Cavendish, the owner of the mansion which he had attempted to rob on the previous night.

Cavendish approached, and inquired if he could have a few minutes' conversation with him.

"That will depend upon the subject of it," replied Paul, whose guilty mind suspected that it must refer to the last night's affair.

"It is rather an unpleasant one, I must admit," answered Edward, "yet having undertaken it, I should fail in my duty were I to omit the present opportunity. You are aware that your attachment to Miss Florence Campbell is displeasing to her friends, and I would know whether terms may not be made by which she will be left free to form a more suitable match."

This proposition did not come unexpectedly to Paul, and he was at no loss for a reply. He had considered with himself that a handsome sum of money would enable him to seek safety abroad without the burden of a woman, whom his callous and selfish heart, though it made a profession, did not really love; and it was with the greatest assurance and coolness possible that he offered, for the sum of two thousand pounds, to free the young lady and her friends from any fear of his company for the future.

Cavendish was startled at the unreasonableness of the sum demanded, and he at once refused to carry such a demand to the major, who, he felt sure, would not listen to it, and who might take it into his head to send the officers to the place of Paul's concealment, and thus consign him to the gallows.

"Let him do this," was Paul's reply, "and he shall rue the consequence. This estate is Flora's, and by her consent am I concealed here. I have letters, too, from her, which shall be published to the world, which will be far from pleasant to the family. If the money is not forthcoming, I have yet sufficient power to induce her to leave her father's home with one who is an outcast, and a fugitive from justice. You know me, Mr. Cavendish, and you know that I will do my best to keep my word. And when you see Miss Campbell," added Paul, "let her understand that it is with no wish of mine that this match is broken off. I am ready to fulfill my promise, and, if she is inclined the same way, we'll be married, in spite of all the obstacles that may be thrown in the way."

CHAPTER XVI.

I prithee hear me, sir,—hear me, I say,
And when my story's ended, you shall judge
If there is not sufficient ground to hate
The wretch I speak of.—Hatred.

ALMOST unconscious as to whither he was directing his footsteps, Edward Cavendish strolled onwards, lost in the labyrinth of his own painful thoughts.

He had reluctantly come to the conclusion that there were no means to avert the much dreaded exposure respecting Florence, except by yielding to the extortionate terms proposed by the fugitive, when a well-known voice startled him from his reverie, and looking up, he saw Mr. Beaumont standing a few paces before him.

"So, so, my young friend," he exclaimed, "I have disturbed you in the midst of your reveries, it seems ; but you must pardon me this once, for I have been wishing for a secret interview like this in order to relate a few facts that may not just at present be made generally known."

"You have not disturbed me," replied Edward ; "for, to speak the truth, my cogitations were just at an end when you spoke to me."

"That's well ; so now tell me if you have leisure to listen to my rigmarole story ; and, mark me, I mean to make it as brief as possible."

"I have nothing at present to occupy my time," answered Edward Cavendish ; and as the old gentleman took his arm, and they proceeded onwards, he thus commenced his narrative :—

"You have heard me say before that, in early life, I entered the army just at a period when a hot war was raging on the peninsula. Of course, like most young men, I was ardent in the profession I had chosen, and ardently did my heart glow when orders were given for my regiment to proceed, without delay, to the scene where the strife was likely to be carried on with the greatest intensity. It is not my intention to weary you with a detail of the various engagements that succeeded our landing in Portugal, but I cannot omit to notice a siege that occupied many weeks of our time, and which was subsequently productive of that misery which has made me more than half a misanthrope. The town I allude to was admirably invested by our forces, and, to do the enemy justice, they defended the place bravely, resolving never to yield whilst they had the power left to defend themselves. At length, however, one of their principal batteries was destroyed by our cannon, and scaling ladders being placed against the walls, we made a desperate attempt to gain an entrance into the town, whatever might be the consequence to our own side. It would make your heart sick were I to recount the scene of slaughter that ensued. Our men fell in hundreds by the hands of those who were determined to defend the place to the last extremity ; and it was not till a breach had been made in the walls, that we were at last enabled to effect an entrance, and then what a fearful scene ensued !—what seas of blood flowed ere the brave enemy was compelled, unconditionally, to surrender ! But I will not dwell on this portion of my narrative—suffice it to say, that the town was given up to the mercy of our infuriated soldiery, who, as is but too frequently the case under such circumstances, gave no quarter to those whose greatest crime was that they had shed much of our blood in their own defence. Struck with horror, I remained a passive observer of all that was going on, and was bitterly regretting that I had joined such a service, when a scream startled me from my dream of horror, and the next moment a female, who was pursued by two of our soldiers, threw herself into my arms for protection."

"And you, of course, saved her from the hands of those merciless ruffians ?" exclaimed Edward.

"I did," replied Mr. Beaumont ; "on my word of command being given, the fellows desisted from the pursuit, and I was left to revive the unfortunate girl who had fainted in my arms."

"Was she young ?"

"She was."

"And beautiful?"

"As an angel."

"And I suppose you afterwards became enamoured of her?"

"I did," replied Mr. Beaumont; "but it was a pure and holy love, such as was merited by such virtue as I found her possessed of."

"Did you marry her?"

"I should have done so," answered the other, "but shortly after quiet was restored in the town I was ordered to head a detachment that was to march, on instant notice, to another part of the country. In this dilemma I had no alternative but to leave her with a brother officer who was to remain behind with the garrison. He had been my schoolfellow, and was, I imagined, my friend; yet, would you believe it, Edward, he was base enough to abuse the trust I had too heedlessly reposed in him?"

"How," asked Edward Cavendish, "did you revenge yourself for such perfidy?"

"The war prevented my meeting with him for some months," replied Mr. Beaumont; "but at length a cessation of hostilities took place, and then, upon making inquiries after the villain, I ascertained that he had proceeded to France. Thither I followed him without a moment's delay, and our meeting may be better imagined by yourself than I can at this moment describe it."

"You challenged him?"

"Ay."

"And slew the destroyer of maiden innocence?"

"He fell by my sword," answered the old gentleman, "and I left him in the belief that he was mortally wounded; such, however, was not the case; he survived the conflict, and, though you would scarcely credit it, 'tis not long since he called to visit me at my own house."

"To offer reparation, I suppose, for the injury he had inflicted?"

"He made no such offer," replied Mr. Beaumont, "but came to make inquiries after the son who was the offspring of his libertine love for the girl he had robbed me of."

"Had he any reason to believe that you could give him information on the subject?" asked Edward.

"At any rate he guessed as much," replied the other; "and he was not very wrong in his surmise, though, from motives of my own, I did not think proper to afford him the clue he desired. But chance soon afterwards threw that son in his way—a discovery took place, and the considerate father, without either revealing who he was, or what his motives were, offered to procure for him a situation under government."

"Surely," cried Edward, with surprise, "in the son I can recognize no other than my excellent young friend, Stephen Harland!"

"The same," answered the other; "I was about to explain as much to you, but your own penetration has saved me the trouble."

"And his mother?"

"Died many years ago," replied Mr. Beaumont. "By a mere accident I heard that she was living in a distant part of England in a state of the most abject destitution. Her faults were forgotten in the deep hatred I bore to the wretch who had plunged her in ruin. I hastened to seek her out, and dreadful indeed was the situation in which I found her and the helpless child she had given birth to!"

"She was deserted, I suppose, by the villain whose lying promises deceived her?"

"You have judged rightly," answered the old gentleman; "and not only did he desert her, but she was left without the means to drag on an existence!"

"Could she not have compelled him to support her?" demanded Edward.

"Such a resource was certainly open to her," exclaimed Mr. Beaumont; "but though she had lost her fair name she had no desire to publish the damning fact to all the world. When forsaken she tried to obtain a precarious livelihood by making fancy articles such as had employed her leisure hours in happier times. But ill-health soon began to manifest itself, and by degrees even this resource began to fail, and to her horror and despair she saw that a workhouse was the only shelter to which she and her child could flee."

"And was it in such an abode that you found her?" asked Edward Cavendish.

"No," replied the other; "luckily she was spared that cruel degradation. I found her just as she had made up her mind to take that step for the sake of her child, and thus preserved her from a fate that she shuddered to think of."

"I can well imagine," exclaimed the young man, "how dreadful must have been the interview that took place between you."

"You can scarcely imagine half the agony with which both of us were afflicted," returned Mr. Beaumont, with a half-suppressed groan. "It were useless to enter further into so painful a subject just now, my dear young friend, and I will therefore merely observe that I heartily forgave the anguish she had occasioned me, and it was finally arranged that she and her infant should return with me, and accept a shelter beneath my roof."

"It was kindly done on your part," said Edward, "but I much doubt whether the world might not construe an act of generosity into one of dishonour."

"Why, some people certainly did think proper to circulate reports to that effect," answered Mr. Beaumont, "and I heeded it no more than if the evil had not been thought or spoken. The truth is, Edward, an approving conscience is our best armour in a case like this, and knowing that my purposes were strictly honourable, I left it for time to prove that my character had been blackened without cause."

"It is not every one," observed Edward, "that could have maintained so much resolution."

"But if every one did so," replied Mr. Beaumont, "the profession of your mischief-maker would have been at an end as a very profitless concern. Besides, the dying condition of the unfortunate woman whom I had thus rescued, was of itself sufficient to disarm scandal of its most poisonous shafts, and as she was shortly afterwards laid in our village churchyard, there were few who could do otherwise than give me the credit of having done a charitable act in receiving her within my doors. To be sure there are persons even to the present day, who believe she had been my mistress at a former period, and that, after casting her off, I had become repentant, and so brought her here to pass away the last few hours of her existence."

"Ah!" exclaimed Edward, "then now I begin to see why people have sometimes thrown out hints in my presence, that Stephen Harland was a son of yours."

"That is a story so often told, that I have grown quite used to it," answered the old gentleman. "You, however, are now in possession of the facts, and I care not what anybody else thinks, since no harm can come of it. Stephen Harland has also learned the chief particulars relating to his parentage, and as he intends to seek an immediate interview with Lord Danebury, it is likely the whole affair may be made public in a shorter time than you imagine."

"Do you intend to accompany him in this visit to his lordship?" asked the other.

"It is my most earnest desire never to see his lordship again," answered Mr. Beaumont. "We can only meet as enemies, and both of us are now too old to plunge into unseemly wrath. Not that I shall ever try to avoid him, and as it is my intention to accompany Stephen to London, a necessity may arise for my seeing Lord Danebury once more."

"When do you and Stephen leave us?"

"This day week."

"May I ask if your sole purpose in going is to obtain this meeting?"

"It is," replied Mr. Beaumont; "his lordship, it seems, begins to feel that he ought to do something for his long neglected son, and, being a strict observer of economy, he intends to do it with as little expense to himself as possible. A government situation is to be procured, and with that it is expected Stephen is to be content. But here, sir, our roads branch off in opposite directions. I thank you for the attention with which you have heard me, and when next we meet, I trust I shall have favourable intelligence to relate of your friend."

Shaking Edward by the hand, they parted, and each pursued his own way home.

CHAPTER XVII.

On certain terms I'll take thee to my heart,
Acknowledge thee my son—ay, exalt thee
Till thou becom'st the envy of that world,
Which now doth coldly look on thee.—*Ambition.*

THE expiration of a week saw Stephen Harland and his friend Mr. Beaumont in London, whither they had gone in pursuance of the intention explained in the foregoing chapter. On the morning after their arrival, they set forth on their way to the square in which Lord Danebury resided, for though Mr. Beaumont did not mean to enter the house of the man he had so much cause to hate, he thought it better to accompany Stephen.

At length they reached the neighbourhood of his lordship's hotel, and as Stephen reluctantly went towards the house, Mr. Beaumont watched him with the anxiety of a parent who was about to part for ever from his only child.

In the meanwhile Stephen reached the mansion, and having presented his card, was conducted to an apartment furnished with all the luxury that appertains only to great wealth. His lordship was not there, but while Stephen was gazing round him with a sensation of wonder and surprise, the owner entered, and receiving his salute with a stiff, formal air, desired him to be seated. Lord Danebury then took some little pains to ascertain that no intruders were present, and being satisfied on that point, he said, as he threw himself into an easy chair,—

" I have the honour, I believe, of addressing myself to Mr. Stephen Harland?"

The youth was piqued at the coldness with which these words were uttered, and for a moment he hesitated whether to make a reply or leave his lordship to proceed with his next question. At length, however, observing that the nobleman waited a reply, he slightly bowed his head in token of assent.

" The name," added his lordship, " is, I believe, an assumed one?"

" It is."

" Do you know from whom you received it?"

" I do not," replied Stephen ; " a mystery that attended my birth has followed me through life ; and I was in hopes that it was your lordship's intention during the present interview, to supply me with the information I require."

" You certainly had no right to expect anything of the kind, sir," exclaimed Lord Danebury, with some severity of tone. " It is true I have taken some little notice of you, and would exert my interest in your behalf ; but why you should expect any explanation from me, I am at a loss to discover."

" You were acquainted with my mother, I believe?"

" I admit that," he replied ; " she was from Portugal ; and, as I have heard, died many years ago. In fact, I believe you lost her during your infancy."

" Alas ! my lord," cried Stephen, " such was, indeed, my cruel misfortune."

" And afterwards," continued the nobleman, " you found a friend in Mr. Beaumont?"

" He was not my first protector," answered Stephen ; " for my earliest years were passed under the guardianship of our vicar. It is true, I have sometimes thought that I was placed under his charge by Mr. Beaumont, but am not certain upon the point."

" I know," exclaimed his lordship, " that you are aware that I am your father ; and you, of course, also know that you are illegitimate ; nay, you need not feel angry at being reminded of it, for I have no unkind motive in alluding to a blemish, the fault of which belongs rather to your parents than to yourself."

" Your lordship," returned Stephen, with ill-suppressed agitation, " is so far considerate."

" It is my wish," replied Lord Danebury, " that there should be no unkindly feeling between us. Like yourself, I have reason to believe that Mr. Beaumont is the friend to whom you are indebted for so many benefits, and would, if possible, be satisfied whether my suspicions are right or wrong."

"My lord," exclaimed Stephen, "I have questioned him frequently upon the subject, but he has always found means to evade my inquiry. He is not fond of blazoning his own good deeds, and whether he has from the first been my benefactor or not, will never be acknowledged by him."

"But you believe your obligations to be due to him, if I rightly understand?"

"I feel almost certain of it."

"And I suppose you feel grateful to him?"

"How, my lord, can I do otherwise?"

"I asked a question, and did not expect one to be put to me in return," cried Lord Danebury, haughtily. "From what I know of this Mr. Beaumont, he can be no real friend of yours; there must be some motive for what he has done for you that exceeds my comprehension, and it therefore need not excite surprise if I feel anxious lest he should be playing a deep game towards you under the mask of friendship."

"Really, my lord," exclaimed Stephen, "I cannot listen to slander against a man whom I have reason to esteem above all others."

"You are young and ignorant of the world's ways," replied Lord Danebury, "and it is therefore easy to find excuse for this warmth in favour of one whom I regard with suspicion. But setting this subject aside, I am now willing to render you a permanent service if it should prove that you are deserving of it. Your education, I understand, has been carefully attended to, and the gift has not been thrown away upon you. So far you are rendered fit for some useful occupation, and as I am not without patronage, you may reckon upon my influence whenever you think proper to ask it."

"I am truly grateful, my lord," answered Stephen, "and another time I may solicit the favour you have offered. At present, however, I am satisfied with the kindness bestowed on me by Mr. Beaumont, and it would appear ungrateful to remove myself from his roof unless it should be manifest that he desires it."

"I shall not command your obedience, sir," returned Lord Danebury, "because I hope a short time will serve to convince you that it were better to depend upon the assistance of a parent than the uncertain kindness proffered by a stranger. However, I would ask you one other question—do you know of anybody else who may have bestowed upon you all these benefits for which Mr. Beaumont is receiving the full credit?"

"I have other kind friends," answered Stephen, "but among them all there is not one who I believe has done these services to me."

"Well," returned Lord Danebury, "I am myself inclined to believe that Mr. Beaumont is the man you have to thank thus far, but, on the other hand, I have to warn you that your expectations must not go further than while he lives. Years may begin to press heavily upon him, and when he quits this world you will find yourself dependant on the terms I have offered, but which you have thought proper to reject."

"And if I have done so," exclaimed Stephen, "it is because the education which has been bestowed upon me has been the means of raising me above the servile employment of which you have spoken."

"Indeed!—may I ask, then, to what you have the ambition to aspire?"

"An honourable profession," answered the young man, proudly.

"Which among them have you fixed your mind upon?" asked his lordship, with a sneer.

"I am indifferent, so that the employment is a useful one to my country."

"I suppose you would prefer either the army or the navy?"

"My thoughts have indeed been directed towards each of them, my lord."

"Then let them be turned any other way," exclaimed Lord Danebury; "for never, with my consent, shall you enter either of the services."

"May I inquire your reason?" asked Stephen.

"For one plain and simple reason," answered the nobleman. "In the army and navy men are apt to be too inquisitive respecting the birth and parentage of those who receive commissions, and as I have no desire that the connexion between you

and us should be known to all the world, I shall most decidedly object to your entering either the army or the navy."

"This, methinks, savours somewhat of tyranny!" exclaimed Stephen; "and I am not yet quite certain whether I can yield implicit obedience even to the commands of a parent."

"How, sir!—dare you rebel?"

"When driven to it I have no alternative," replied the young man, in a tone of decision. "Till lately I have been neglected by him who should have been my protector, and now, scarcely has he thought proper to recognize me, than he exercises a command over me that I have not been used to. Such has never been the conduct of my former friends, and therefore am I the less inclined to submit now."

"Come, there's some spirit in you, at all events," cried Lord Danebury, "and that alone is sufficient to disarm me of half my anger. You must, however, submit in some degree to my control, and I dare say we shall understand each other very well before long. I would serve you, Stephen, and it will be your own fault if we do not very soon get upon a better footing."

"What further conditions have you to insist on?" asked Stephen Harland.

"There is one of paramount importance," answered Lord Danebury; "you must henceforth renounce this Mr. Beaumont as a man of whom the greatest doubts are to be entertained."

"Doubts!"

"Ay; is he not my foe—and should my son prefer his society to my own?"

"He has been as a father to me," replied Stephen, pointedly, "when my own parent deigned not to acknowledge the wretched being to whom he had given existence."

"Your reproach may be partly founded in justice," answered his lordship; "yet I must warn you to be careful how you judge my motives, since there were reasons for my conduct which I am not at liberty to explain at the present moment. I have never ceased to think of you with affection, and at the first opportunity commenced a personal inquiry, which at length led to my finding you in the neighbourhood of my friend, Major Campbell."

"Your request is most unjust," replied Stephen. "I have received the greatest benefits from Mr. Beaumont, and yet, in consequence of some private quarrel of your own with him, you would now have me prove ungrateful to a generous benefactor. My lord, I cannot comply with it."

"I will hear no more," cried Lord Danebury, rising, angrily, from his seat; "your disobedience has been sufficiently manifested, and we have seen each other for the last time, unless you yield to my commands."

Darting an angry frown at Stephen Harland, the haughty nobleman instantly quitted the room.

For a few moments, Stephen remained gazing with ill-suppressed indignation upon the door through which Lord Danebury had disappeared, and then he also rose, and prepared to leave the house.

A servant was in waiting to show him to the door, and, with every mark of civility and respect, he was conducted to the hall.

As he descended the steps, Stephen fancied that the features of Lord Danebury were discernible at one of the upper windows, watching his departure with a much kinder expression than it had wore during their prolonged interview. This gave rise to conflicting and agitating emotions, and he moved from the spot in a much better frame of mind.

CHAPTER XVIII.

A friend
Ingenuous, noble, faithful, generous,
E'en but to look at him had been full warrant
Against the accusing tongue of man or angel,
To all the world beside—
A friend whose fostering love had been the stay,
The guide, the solace of his wayward youth,—
Love steady, tried, unwearied,—
A friend who, in his best devoted thoughts,
His happiness in earth, his bliss in heaven,
Intwined his image, and could naught desire
Of separate good.—JOANNA BAILLIE.

ON reaching the hotel, whither Mr. Beaumont had returned, and entering the apartment occupied by himself and his friend, Stephen Harland found Mr. Beaumont anxiously awaiting his return; and scarcely had he made his appearance in the room than the old gentleman, grasping him eagerly by the hand, demanded if he had seen Lord Danebury.

"I have," was the laconic reply.

"If I had happened to have been one of your sporting men," exclaimed Mr. Beaumont, "I should not mind betting a cool hundred that your meeting has ended in a very pretty quarrel."

"You have exactly guessed it, sir," replied Stephen. "His lordship thought proper to be rather peremptory in certain demands that he made, and as I did not choose to accede to them, he began to regard me as an undutiful son, and the consequence was that we parted upon worse terms than we had met."

"I can guess what it was all about," said the old gentleman, after a little consideration. "His lordship has no very great liking for me, and he would persuade you to quit my roof, because he knows that such a course is most likely to occasion me the greatest pain. Am I not about right, Stephen Harland?"

"That was, indeed, the subject of our difference," replied the young man. "He acknowledged, too, that there was a long-standing quarrel between you, and, from certain words that escaped him, I could discover that he never has, and never will, forgive you."

"Did he acquaint you with the origin of our quarrel?" demanded Mr. Beaumont, eagerly.

"He did not," replied the other; "and I have, therefore, to request from you an explanation of the ill-feeling that exists between you."

"Do not ask it at present," exclaimed the old gentleman, earnestly.

"May I ask if I am in any way connected with it ?"

"You are, Stephen—you are," answered Mr. Beaumont, with emotion. "Your mother's name and fame will suffer, should this affair be talked about, and, for her sake, I conjure you to pursue this inquiry no further at present."

"May I ask an explanation at a future time ?"

"Ay," he replied ; "and I may then no longer see any reason to withhold it, though, to confess the truth, I would much rather the affair was suffered to remain as it is."

"But it would be most unjust to me if it should do so," returned Stephen ; "for you have acknowledged that I have an interest in it, and I may, therefore, surely demand an explanation whenever you think proper to give it me ; for his lordship, though my father, it must be admitted I feel very little respect, and, that being the case, you need be under no apprehension about widening the breach that has already been commenced between us."

"You have not yet told me," said Mr. Beaumont, wishing to change the subject of their conversation, "whether his lordship said anything more about the situation he was to provide you with."

"Oh ! yes," replied Stephen ; "he mentioned it, and seemed to think it a matter of course that I should accept his very generous offer."

"And you did not do so ?"

"I gave him no absolute refusal," replied the young man ; "but the conversation turned to the old grudge that existed between you and him, and, as we afterwards parted upon very indifferent terms, there is, of course, an end of the very magnificent views that he entertained relative to my future advancement in life."

"So much the better," exclaimed Mr. Beaumont ; "for now, my dear boy, there can be no longer a reason why you should leave me. I am a rough, plain-spoken old man, that has made more enemies than friends by speaking the honest truth, when, to please the world, I ought to have acted the part of a hypocrite. You, however, know and can bear with me ; we have known each other long enough to form a pretty accurate opinion, and if you will promise henceforth to become the sharer of my dwelling, you shall, at my death, be placed beyond the cold charity of this proud lord, whom you have the misfortune to call father."

"Words cannot express the gratitude I feel at the generous offer you have made, sir," cried Stephen, affected by the kindness thus manifested towards him by one who might almost be regarded in the light of a stranger. I would fain convey to you the deep sense I entertain of your intentions towards me, but, at the same time, I must declare to you that I should take shame to myself were I to pursue a life of indolence when means have been afforded me to push my own way in the world."

"Would you leave me, then, Stephen?" demanded the old gentleman, dejectedly.

"Only for a time, sir," he replied. "To your kindness I was indebted for all the comforts of this life, and I would now go forth and seek some honourable profession, in which I may earn the applause and respect of my fellow-creatures."

"Ah !" exclaimed Mr. Beaumont, "I dare say all this is said with the very best of intentions, but you speak like a young man, as you are, who has had no experience of life to boast of ; you seem altogether to have forgotten the peculiar circumstances of this case. I took you into my house, and a regard such as exists between some parents and their children rose up between us. I am a bachelor, without relatives, am tolerably rich, and, since some one must inherit what I leave behind, I see no reason why you should not be my heir as well as anybody else. So now, Stephen, what say you?—am I to have your consent, or will you make me a wretched old man for the remainder of my days ?"

"Really, my dear sir," cried Stephen, "you have taken me so much by surprise that I know not how to answer till I have considered your proposition."

"I can see clearly enough what stands in the way," exclaimed Mr. Beaumont, after a short pause. "I have cautioned you on several occasions against falling in love ; but the words of an old man were unheeded, and, having given your heart to Laura Campbell, you are afraid of encountering my opposition to your union."

"I had scarcely time to give that affair a thought," replied Stephen, smiling at the old man's singular fancy ; "but since you have, in some respect, forced the subject, I will candidly confess that I would endure no restraint were I but assured that her love is bestowed upon me ?"

"How can you doubt it," asked Mr. Beaumont, "when even an old man like me can see it plainly enough with half an eye ?"

"You may be deceived, sir."

"And *you* most certainly are if you think she loves anybody else."

"I am afraid she does," replied Stephen.

"Hilloa ! what's in the wind now ?" exclaimed the old gentleman. "Has the demon of jealousy got hold of you, that I hear you talking in this unusual fashion, Stephen Harland ?"

"Why, the truth is, my dear sir," answered Stephen, "I love Miss Campbell so well that I cannot endure the thought of her becoming the wife of any other man."

"Indeed ; and have you any reason to suspect such a thing as being possible ?"

"I have had my doubts."

"Humph ! May I inquire who is the rival that you suspect of a design to carry off your mistress ?"

"You treat the affair very lightly, sir, but the truth is, lovers are ——"

"Very foolish fellows," interrupted Mr. Beaumont. "I admit it, sir—I admit it ; so now come to the point at once. Who, let me ask, is the gentleman whose rivalry you suspect ?"

"One whom I regard," answered Stephen, "and whom I can acquit of any deliberate intention to do me an injury ; in fact, he is no other than my friend, Edward Cavendish."

"Mr. Edward Cavendish !" exclaimed the old gentleman ; "why, you must have taken leave of your senses, my dear fellow."

"I am willing to hope that I am mistaken," replied Stephen ; "but, let that be as it may, Edward Cavendish has lately visited the house of Major Campbell a great deal more frequently than ever he did before, and I could only attribute the circumstance to his having conceived a passion for Laura."

"Well, upon my word, you lovers take a vast deal of pains to torture yourselves," exclaimed Mr. Beaumont. "You see something very alarming in these visits paid to the house where you are yourself, at all times, a welcome guest ; and I see nothing more in it than a likelihood that Edward has taken a fancy to Florence Campbell, who, if I have been rightly informed, may yet be induced to give up that reprobate lover of hers, Paul Rayland, or Paul the Reckless, as they sometimes call him."

"Do you indeed think Edward's visits are intended for Florence instead of her sister, as I suspected ?" asked Stephen, as if just waking from a dream.

"Why, I not only think so, but I'm sure of it," replied Mr. Beaumont. "We both of us know Edward Cavendish well enough to be certain that he would not be guilty of a treacherous act against his friend ; and no one but a jealous lover would ever have suspected that his visits to the Clock-house were prompted by any other motives than to see and converse with the pretty Florence Campbell."

"I begin to think as you do about it," replied Stephen ; "and yet, for all that, I cannot quite convince myself that she has dismissed Paul Rayland, who she believed was fondly attached to her, though, the truth is, he was only trying to make what he fancied would be an excellent bargain for himself."

"Ay," answered Mr. Beaumont, "but the fellow has been since told the exact situation of affairs, and now that he finds she will not have so large a fortune as he expected, he is willing to accept a sum of money on the express condition that he is never to show his face in that part of the country again."

"Which condition," observed the young man, "he will either keep or break according as it may suit his purpose."

"That there is no great reliance to be placed in his word I admit," replied Mr. Beaumont; "but, at the same time, it must not be forgotten that he has laid himself open to the law, and it is only by remaining tolerably quiet that he can hope to remain at liberty. So I think Florence may consider herself quite safe from his future persecution, and something strikes me that Edward Cavendish will lead her to the altar on the very same day that her sister Laura vows to love, honour, and obey you."

Stephen Harland made no immediate reply to this, and when next the conversation was resumed Mr. Beaumont turned it into another channel. In fact, as their business in London had been brought to a termination sooner than was expected, they arranged to return home next morning.

CHAPTER XIX.

Is thy heart turned to stone,
That thou canst see, unmoved, a woman's grief?
Shame on thee, recreant! Hie thee hence,
For thou art less than man.—*Marianne.*

It is now time that we should return to Paul Rayland, who still lurked about the ruined fishing temple watching for Patty, who frequently wandered thither to look for Richard Elliot, who had chosen that spot as their place of meeting, because they were less likely to be interrupted. On the evening in question, she took an opportunity to stroll unperceived from the house, and having taken a circuitous route, to avoid meeting any of the gossiping neighbours, she at length reached the exterior of the building; but no Richard Elliot was there, and her heart sank within her as a thousand jealous fancies crowded thickly upon her imagination.

Yet, when she came to reflect more dispassionately upon the subject, she thought it hardly likely he would prove false to his oft-repeated promises, and as there was a possibility that he might be inside the building, she pushed open the door, and ascending the flight of steps that led to the upper portion of the structure, entered the cheerless, unfurnished chamber where, on a former occasion, she had met her lover when a sudden storm had compelled them to take shelter there. As she moved forward, a footstep in advance caused her to look up in the expectation that Elliot was there before her, but the consternation of the poor girl may be imagined when, instead of beholding her lover, she saw the dark, ill-omened form of Paul Rayland glowering upon her, like a demon exulting over the prey that has fallen into his hands. Startled at the sight, she uttered a piercing cry of terror, and was retreating, in order to make her escape, when Paul, springing past her, secured the door, and then, after giving utterance to a hollow laugh of triumph, demanded what she was so greatly alarmed at.

"I—I did not expect to meet *you* here," she stammered.

"That you need scarcely have told me," answered Paul; "but as I expected to meet you here, I suppose it's all the same thing in the end. So, with your good leave, pretty one, I'll help myself to a kiss, just by way of convincing you that there's no occasion to be afraid of me."

"Ruffian, stand off!" cried Patty, snatching from the floor a long-bladed knife, which he had just before dropped, and holding the weapon threateningly in her hand, she stood resolved to defend herself should he advance another step.

"Come, come, Patty," he said, coaxingly, when he thus saw that she had him at an advantage; "I was only joking with you, girl; so throw away the knife, child, and then, if you will allow me, I'll see you a part of the way towards home, for it's a dull road, and ——"

"I want none of your company," she exclaimed; "and, what's more, I'm determined not to trust myself with a ruffian that has not honour enough to respect a female when he believes she is without a protector."

"Well," he exclaimed, "at any rate, I suppose you won't use that ugly weapon against me?"

"That will depend upon yourself," she replied. "I am not likely to commit a murder without provocation, but the moment you attempt to lay hands upon me, either you or I perish."

"Upon my life, you are a very devil in spirit," exclaimed Paul, with affected carelessness. "I thought there was no great harm in kissing a pretty girl, but you make as much fuss about it as if there were a hundred pair of eyes looking upon us."

"I'll tell you what it is, Master Paul Rayland," answered Patty, "your character is well known, and no female was ever seen in your company but she's set down at once as being as bad as yourself."

"Indeed!" he exclaimed; "then the world must speak badly enough of Florence Campbell, for scarcely a day passes but what she condescends to pay me a visit here."

"The more fool she, to trust herself, and the greater rogue you, to brag about it," retorted Patty. "I have heard something of her meeting you when she ought to have been in her own comfortable home, but it don't follow that she is always such a simpleton as to give up the happiness of her life for the sake of a worthless ruffian like you."

"These are hard words, Patty, to use to a man that you cannot prove to be a ruffian."

"I can prove that the words are no harder than you deserve," she replied; "and, if what I say is not agreeable, you had better let me go my ways, and then there will be an end of it."

"We must have a little further chat, my dear, before we part," replied Paul, with his usual cool indifference. "You have called me a villain, and sundry other vile names, and I should like to know in what way I have merited them."

"In more ways than one," she retorted; "have you forgot your attack on young Mr. Stephen Harland, only because you fancied he visited the Clock-house to see Miss Florence Campbell?"

"Ay, ay, that's true enough," exclaimed Paul. "I certainly did handle him rather roughly; but surely that may be excused, since my anger was roused by the thought that he was about to rob me of a prize that was intended for my-self."

"You may make what excuse you please about it," replied Patty, "but there's a warrant out against you for it, and should the officers happen to trace you out, I'm thinking you would be likely to meet your deserts."

"Would you be the one to tell them where to find me?"

"That's impossible," she replied, "for you have taken care to prevent it by locking the door, and making a prisoner of me."

"But suppose I set you at liberty?"

"Why, then I don't know what I should do."

"Might I rely on your keeping the secret of my being here, in consideration of being permitted to depart freely from the place?"

"I shall make no promise of the sort," answered the girl; "it is true I am a prisoner here, and that, too, in company that is not very pleasant; but then I am luckily armed, and, perhaps, as safe as if I was at liberty. But I warn you of one thing, Paul Rayland—I shall soon be missed, and if my Richard comes to look after me, and finds us in each other's company, I would have you look to yourself."

"Richard! What, you mean your lover, I suppose?"

"Yes, my lover," she replied; "but not such a lover as you are, that would insult a helpless woman, when he thinks she has not the means to protect herself from your villany."

"Patty," exclaimed the fugitive, "let me intreat of you to cease these reproaches. I have done wrong—I know I have—but what can a man do more than acknowledge his fault?"

"Why, the next thing you ought to do is to turn the key of yonder door, and set me at liberty."

"But I must ask a favour in return."

"What is it?"

"A kiss, you little rogue—nay, never look so cross at me, girl—I told you at first what I wanted, and if you had not made so much fuss about it, you might have had your liberty half an hour ago."

"I shall make no reply to your insult," she exclaimed; "but it may be as well to warn you against that which may cost you your life. I am still armed, Paul Rayland, and if you dare lay hands upon me, I will bury this blade to its very haft in your body."

"Would you become a murderer?"

"I will protect myself at all hazards."

"But surely you would not take away the life of the man that loves you?"

"You love me not," she exclaimed, passionately, "or never would a word of insult have escaped your lips."

"My dear girl, you mistake me."

"Indeed, but I do no such thing," she replied. "I take you to be a villain, and all your ingenuity will never serve to convince me that I am wrong."

"Surely," he exclaimed, "there can be no crime in falling in love with a pretty wench."

"Your flattery is thrown away upon me," retorted Patty; "for there is only one person that I ever care about paying me compliments, and he has left it off since he found out that I had no fancy for any such unmeaning rubbish."

"Then he's a fool for his pains," exclaimed Paul, "for in my own experience I have always seen that the best way to reach a girl's heart, is to praise her beauty. I care nothing for their denying it, because I have always seen that if you leave off praising their good looks, they at once believe you are growing cold towards them, and it's a hundred to one if they don't look round for another lover."

"Hark!" cried Patty, as a noise was heard below, like some one trying to force the door, which she had closed as she had entered the ruin. Paul remained silent a few minutes, and then, as nothing more was heard, he held out his hand to Patty, and in his blandest accents, exclaimed,—

"Come, come, my dear girl, don't let us keep this distance from each other, but throw away that ugly tool, and trust yourself to the honour of a man that will never deceive you."

"That I'll dare be sworn you never will," answered Patty; "because I don't mean to give you an opportunity, now that I know what sort of a fellow you are. But, come, Mister Paul Rayland, you have carried on this game quite long enough, I think, so be pleased to open the door, before I scream out, and disturb the neighbourhood."

"Disturb the neighbourhood!" returned the other; "no one would be likely to hear you, and even if they did, I should like to know who would ever think of coming to this place to seek for you?"

"Villain!" she cried, "you think, then, I am in your power, and that nothing on earth can rescue me from it."

"I am sure of it, my girl," he replied; "so kiss me, like a good wench, and then, perhaps, I may let you go for the present."

"Insolent!" she cried angrily; "approach me another step, and it shall be the last one you ever make on this side the grave!"

"Psha! this is madness," he exclaimed; "my strength is sufficient to protect me from the vain efforts of an infuriated woman, and in one instant I could disarm you."

He made a sudden snatch at the knife as he uttered these words, but she was too quick for him, and stepping back three or four paces nearer to the door, she said,—

"You have tried to take the knife away from me once, and have failed—let me warn you how you make a second attempt, for you may not get off quite so well as you did the first time."

"What can you do without assistance?"

"Thank Heaven here is assistance at hand," cried Patty, as the noise which had startled her before was again heard. "Some one is even now within reach of me, and Paul Rayland shall yet find to his cost that I am not quite so friendless as he just now imagined."

"Psha!" exclaimed the ruffian; "it was but the wind shaking the old door, down below, so don't fill yourself with a parcel of hopes that can only end in disappointment."

"I am right," she ejaculated; "hark! the latch is moved rapidly up and down, and I can hear some one rush with all his force against the door to force it open. There is no deception in this, Paul Rayland, and if you would save your miserable life I advise you to do so now, for in a few moments it will not be easy to do so."

"Without you I stir not," he exclaimed, resolutely.

"Madman!" cried Patty, "think you that I am to be terrified now that I am assured assistance is at hand?"

"Then I have no alternative but this," he exclaimed, seizing her suddenly by the arm, and wrenching from her the knife, which he instantly dashed upon the ground. "Now," he added, "you have no longer the power of resistance; yonder opposite doorway leads to another entrance, from whence I can easily bear you to the Haunted Hollow. Once there you are safe in my power, let who may come forth to rescue you."

"Villain! take that for your reward," shouted Richard Elliot, who at that moment rushed towards them, aiming at the fugitive a tremendous blow with the ponderous bludgeon that he carried in his hand. Luckily for Paul, however, the blow did not take the intended effect, for instead of alighting on his head it fell on his brawny shoulder, felling him to the ground, however, and thus compelling him to let go his hold of Patty, who being released, sprang towards the window, and screamed loudly for assistance.

"Now, villain!" vociferated Richard Elliot, as he knelt over his prostrate foe with the knife in his hand, which had just before been thrown upon the ground; "what have you now to say in your own defence, after threatening and terrifying a poor defenceless girl?"

"I have done no such thing," answered Paul, in a voice almost suffocated with rage. "I was here by chance when she came, and thought there was no great harm in speaking to an old acquaintance."

"She is no old acquaintance of yours," retorted Elliot, "and for half a farthing I would cut your tongue out for the falsehood it has uttered."

"Would you murder a fellow-creature in cold blood?" muttered the fugitive.

"I should think it no very great crime to put you out of the way, at any rate," answered Richard Elliot. "People have told me for some time past, that you were dodging Patty about wherever she went, and I've been keeping a sharp look-out to catch you, with a determination that, whenever we did meet, you should have as pretty a thrashing as ever any fellow had in his life."

"Then give me an equal chance with you, and don't be striking a poor fellow when he's down," muttered Paul, and then watching an opportunity, he was making a spring to regain his feet, when a second blow from his antagonist once more laid him sprawling on the floor. Being thus again defeated, Paul Rayland made a snatch at the knife, but Elliot foresaw it in time, and incensed at the perfidy that was intended, he raised the weapon, and would have plunged it into the body of his foe, had not his arm at the moment been arrested, and looking round, he saw, to his surprise, that Major Campbell and Florence had just entered.

CHAPTER XX.

I will hear your terms—
Speak freely, sir, and state the propositions
On which you will consent to yield the claims
You just now made.—*The Usurer.*

For a few moments, the different parties composing this singular group remained regarding each other intently, possessed by the most varied passions.

Paul Rayland hid his face in his hands, and seemed unable to meet the gaze of either Major Campbell or his daughter, while Richard Elliot released the ruffian from his grasp, and stood silently waiting for the major to speak, and Patty clung to the window, whence she had been calling for assistance, as if overcome by surprise and alarm.

A constrained silence reigned through that desolate summer-house—a silence painful to every one there, and the beating of poor Florence's heart could be heard, as the blood flowed tumultuously through her veins. There she stood, the very image of despair, her hands clasped, her mouth slightly parted, her eyes fixed upon the prostrate form of Paul Rayland, as he cowered before her, and with a death-like hue upon her face, sad to look upon in one so young and beautiful.

When Major Campbell had, in some measure, overcome the surprise the unlooked-for scene had occasioned him, he advanced towards Richard Elliot, and in a stern tone of voice, he exclaimed,—

"What," is the reason of this deadly strife? Speak, Elliot, for from you a least I expect to hear why I have thus found you seeking the life of one who, whatever may be his crimes, has, it seems, sought a shelter within my domains."

"You have asked for the truth, sir, and shall have it," replied Elliot. "The case stands thus—I love Patty, and for a long time past we have been in the habit of meeting each other near this place. Till now, no one has ever disturbed us; but this evening, when I came as usual, Patty was nowhere to be seen, and I was just thinking that I might as well go home again, when I heard her voice, and upon listening, I found that she was being kept here against her will. That, as you must allow, was enough to put my blood up, and bursting open the door, I rushed to her rescue, struck the villain to the ground, and if you had not come in the very nick of time, it's likely Mr. Paul Rayland would have paid the penalty of his crimes."

" Has this man spoken the truth ?" asked Florence, reproachfully. " But I see, Paul, you cannot deny a word that has been alleged against you ; and this, after all, is my reward, for placing reliance in your vows of love. With all your faults I believed your love for me was sincere, yet now do I find that another has shared the heart which you have so often vowed was all my own."

" Ay, rail on," exclaimed Paul, sullenly, " for it's ever the way of the world— if a man's down, every one thinks he has a right to put his foot on him."

" You have brought it all upon yourself, and have, therefore, no right to claim our pity," said Major Campbell. " I have long known you to be a villain, but till this moment I knew not that you had the presumption to pay your addresses to my daughter."

" Presumption," retorted the other ; " is it then so high an honour to seek alliance with the family of Major Campbell, a professed gamester, who has plunged himself and his daughters in ruin ?"

" Your reproaches I deserve," replied the soldier, " and can therefore bear them even from a wretch so debased as yourself. I have, however, seen my madness, and though repentance comes late, I hope there is yet a chance that the ruin you speak of is not so complete as my enemies may wish."

" I, at least, am not to be ranked among your enemies," answered Paul, " for, if I had been inclined, there have been opportunities enough for me to triumph in your downfall. But the truth is, I respected you for the sake of your daughter ; yet, after all, I can listen to your reproaches, and hear myself insulted, for the marvellous great offence of seeking an alliance with your family."

" Florence," cried her father, " did you encourage this man's addresses ?"

" Alas ! I cannot deny it."

" Yet you made no confidant of me."

" How could I do so," she asked, " when I knew the insuperable objections that would be raised against our union. I loved him, and believed his protestations that he had seen the error of his ways, and that I alone possessed the power to bring him once more back to that society whose esteem he had forfeited."

" But now," said her father, " I suppose you have seen and convinced yourself that he was only professing a love to you, which was, in reality, given to another ?"

" I have indeed discovered my error," she replied, " and from henceforth I discard him from my heart, as one that has proved himself unworthy of my love."

" Am I to understand," demanded Paul, haughtily, " that Miss Campbell discards me for no other offence than having been found in company with another female ?"

" You have heard me," she replied, " and having once given my decision, you will find it no easy matter to prevail on me to reverse it."

And so saying, she turned away, and walked to the window, where Patty and Richard Elliot had retired, in order that they might not interfere with what was going forward.

" May I inquire, Major Campbell," said Paul, in a whisper that he did not wish to be overheard, " if you, as well as your daughter, have made up your minds that this shall be no match after all ?"

" Most assuredly."

" Yet you know I am a resolute fellow, and having once made up my mind, I am not to be thwarted without an effort to carry my point."

" Humph ! You would threaten me !"

" I have no wish to do that," replied the other, carelessly ; " but I thought it as well to give you a hint that it would be better to give your consent freely than to have her carried off by force, whether you like it or not."

" Ruffian !"

"Come, come—civil words, if you please, major," returned Paul Rayland. "I am not one of those that yield for slight obstacles that may be thrown in my way; and now, once for all, I tell you that if Florence Campbell is not to be my wife, she shall never be the bride of any other man."

"Insolent scoundrel! what am I to understand by that threat?"

"That sooner than she shall give her hand to a rival," answered Paul, with a fierce scowl, "I would have her heart's blood."

"Wretch!" exclaimed Major Campbell, "dare you utter this language to one who has afforded you a shelter when no other place of refuge was to be found by the guilty fugitive?"

"The shelter was not *given* to me, for I took it without asking leave," replied the other, coldly. "You knew not of my presence here, or it is likely I should have found another sort of shelter in the county gaol, if you had had your own way."

"The language you have held to me this night is enough to convert me into a bitter enemy," returned the major. "However, I would rather that we should part as friends than enemies, and if you think proper to take your departure from hence without delay, I will promise that no pursuit shall be made till you are far enough out of reach."

"That would be a very good bargain for yourself," answered Paul, "but a very indifferent one for me. I have been wooing your daughter for some months, and with what success our frequent stolen interviews will best prove. In fact, major, I had every reason to felicitate myself upon the honour of being received into your family, and I, therefore, leave you to judge whether it is very likely I shall give up my advantage without receiving something or other by way of recompense."

"What do you expect?"

"Money."

"To what amount?"

"That shall be agreed upon between us presently."

"And on condition that your terms are agreed to, you will give up all further claim to my daughter?"

"For a time I will; but then it must be on her promise not to marry anybody else till the period we may name has expired."

"That is a condition," observed Major Campbell, "that I think neither I nor my daughter are ever likely to agree to."

"Then, having her written promise of marriage, I shall hold her to the bargain."

"And a very indifferent bargain you will make of it," said the major; "for my daughter's marriage portion will be an exceedingly small one, and your thirst for gold, which has thus urged you on, will end in disappointment."

"Not at all," he replied; "I have heard that Florence has no great expectations, and was, consequently, prepared to take her with whatever fortune may belong to her. It was my intention to take her abroad to some part of the continent, where a little money goes a great way. However, as it seems the marriage is not agreeable to her friends, I am willing to postpone it for any reasonable time, but it must be on condition that I receive a sum of money immediately to enable me to leave England without delay."

"Will fifty pounds satisfy you?"

"'Tis a small sum for so great a sacrifice," replied the other. "The girl has loved me, and is bound to me by her own written words, though you would fain persuade her that the marriage is a disgraceful one. But man may repent the evil of his ways, Major Campbell, and become, in appearance, a respectable member of society."

"True," replied the other, thoughtfully; "but we have not yet any proof that your repentance will be sincere. Leave this country for a couple of years—even then you and Florence will both be young, and if, at the expiration of that time, you return an altered man, and the marriage is desired by both of you, I pledge myself that no further obstacle shall be thrown in your way."

" Have I your solemn word for this ?"

" You have."

" Am I to receive fifty pounds ?"

" Ay ; that was the offer I made."

" When will you give it me ?"

" Directly ; I have just that sum about me, and it shall be yours ; but, mind, you must leave this place with the first appearance of daylight to-morrow morning."

" Ay, ay—never fear," exclaimed Paul Rayland ; and clutching the purse that Major Campbell offered, he thrust it into his pocket, with a low chuckle of exultation.

" I believe our business is now settled," cried the major ; "and I have only to add, that, if you keep your part of the bargain, I will not fail to keep mine. Farewell ; and should we meet again in two years' time, let me hope that it will be to find you an altered and a better man."

Major Campbell now led his daughter away, without allowing her a parting word with her worthless lover ; and, being closely followed by Patty and Richard Elliot, they left the ruin, glad to escape from the presence of him who was now its only inmate.

———

CHAPTER XXI.

Thus villany doth meet its just reward ;
And he who plots against his fellow man,
Falls, unlamented—cursed—dishonoured !—*The Venetian.*

AFTER passing hours of restless anxiety, Paul Rayland stole, at earliest daybreak, from the ruin, and scarcely heeding whither he directed his steps, pursued his way towards the Haunted Hollow. His countenance was haggard and careworn, for, in spite of his usual recklessness, a weight seemed to oppress his brain, and a sort of superstitious feeling took possession of his soul that seemed to warn him of impending evil. Still he pursued his way through the well-known tracks of the place that had so often afforded him a shelter ; but in vain did he look around for Rough Rob, whom he was anxious to see ; and at length, reaching a place where a mound of earth had been raised, he threw himself upon it, to indulge the more freely in those thoughts which were rushing tumultuously through his brain.

He had been here, perhaps, half an hour, when his reflections were disturbed by the sound of approaching footsteps, and starting up from the place on which he had thrown himself, he confronted the very man of whom he had been in search.

" You are an early riser this morning, Paul," said the new-comer ; "but, perhaps, there are reasons for it that you don't choose to tell me."

" It can't remain a secret much longer, Rob," answered the other ; "and I may as well tell you at once that I've grown tired of this sort of life, and am going abroad to see if I can't find a little more liberty than I've enjoyed of late."

" Ugh ! going abroad, eh ?—and what's to become of the girl you've been a courting so long ?"

" That is a question you and I must talk about presently," replied Paul. "The truth is, I've seen old Major Campbell, and as he don't seem to have any great fancy for my marrying his daughter, he has given me a sum of money on condition that I don't see her for two years."

" And so you mean to keep your promise ?"

" I believe not," replied the other, "for I already begin to repent the bargain ; and if you like to help me, I don't know but she may be persuaded to accompany me in spite of all her father has said against it."

" When are you to leave us ?"

" This very day, if I keep strictly to the terms of our agreement."

" Humph ! and how are you to persuade the girl to leave home at such a short notice ?"

" Why, I was thinking," replied Paul, "that we might do a little something before I go, by way of fixing the date of my departure in the memory of the people hereabouts. In short, my friend, I have planned a robbery, and ——"

" A robbery!—are you mad ?"

" Have patience, I pray, and hear me out," exclaimed Paul. " I don't half like leaving this girl behind me, so I was thinking that as it's still early morning we might pay a visit to the Clock-house, and while I am engaged in persuading Florence to become the partner of my journey, you may occupy yourself in picking and choosing a few of the valuables about the place, which we shall be able to divide between us at some spot that we may appoint for that purpose."

" And you would run all this risk for a girl that, perhaps, don't care anything about you ?"

" But I tell you she does care about me," exclaimed Paul, " and the prize would have been mine long ago, if it had not been for a parcel of busy fools that thought proper to tell her all sorts of things to my prejudice. Hasn't she met me over and over again at night, when there was no fear of any one disturbing us? And who was it but she that gave me shelter in the old ruin when the search of those plaguy constables made this place too hot to hold us ?"

" Well, I suppose you know best about that," answered Rob, sullenly; " but it seems her father wants to get rid of you, and depend on it this place will never do for you to remain in if his daughter should be taken away from his house."

" I don't intend to remain here," answered Paul. " She would follow me all over the world, I believe, and if I once persuade her to elope it shall not be many hours before we find our way over to the continent. I have money enough for that, and if cash should grow short afterwards I can join with a party of smugglers that I know on the coast of Normandy, and there you can make one of us if you like to come over."

" Paul," exclaimed the other, fiercely; " I have always known you for a reckless fellow, but now I have discovered you to be a villain !"

" Ha !" vociferated the fugitive; " are you against me like all the rest of the world ?"

" I was never much for you, that I know of," answered Rob, in a tone of defiance. " To suit my own purposes I have avoided coming to an open quarrel, but now it's time we should understand each other, and I again tell you to your teeth that you are a villain."

" I know it," replied Paul; " but tell me in what way I have ever been a villain to you."

" Not directly to me, perhaps," answered the other; " but you acted the part of a scoundrel to one that I loved better than all the world beside."

" Ah ! I understand—you want to renew our quarrel about Susan Tripley."

" You know my meaning then, it seems," exclaimed Rob. " Yes, yes; it is of her I am speaking; she, poor girl, that trusted you and was betrayed, though you swore by your soul that she should be made your honest wife."

" I did so," replied Rob; " but if she took it into her head to die, was that any fault of mine ?"

" The poor wench died of a broken heart," exclaimed the other; " you put her off from time to time with all sorts of excuses, and when it came to be quite plain that all your promises were worth nothing, the sorrowing girl drooped till she was brought to the grave on which I just now found you sitting."

" Is this the grave of Susan Tripley ?" exclaimed the fugitive, as with a trembling hand he pointed to the mound which, but a few minutes before, had been his resting-place.

" It is," answered Rob; " there lies the wreck of her you deceived. I loved, and would have wedded her, had not you, like a demon of mischief, come between us to blight all the fair prospects we had pictured to ourselves. She died in my presence, and I forgave the wrong she had done me, but never have I forgiven you, Paul Rayland, though it has suited my own purposes to conceal my hatred till this moment."

" And why have you chosen this moment to pick a quarrel with me ?"

"Because it seems you are about to quit England, and it is likely we may never meet again to settle the differences between us."

"You are rash to urge me thus, Rob!"

"It is my humour to do so," replied the other. "Thus far we have been companions in all sorts of crime, but my only motive for keeping about this place was, that I might never lose sight of you."

"But you are likely to do so now," replied Paul, carelessly, "unless you think proper to accompany me over the water."

"You will never leave England, Paul."

"Indeed! for once you will prove a bad prophet; I am now on my way to the coast, and if there is not a vessel that's going to sail directly, I mean to hire an open boat and cross over to France without further ceremony."

"That," exclaimed Rob, "will depend upon whether I choose to let you."

"You let me!"

"Ay, you may sneer," retorted the other, "but I can hinder it if I think proper. The death of Susan Tripley has never been forgotten or forgiven; I vowed to revenge her fate, and if my oath has not been fulfilled before now, it was because I knew you were in my power, and I could execute my purpose whenever I liked. In my own mind it was resolved that you should perish on the spot where she found her last earthly resting-place. Paul Rayland, you now stand with one foot upon the grave of your victim, and thus do I avenge the death of the unfortunate girl whose heart and hopes you blighted!"

Whilst he was speaking, Rob drew a pistol from beneath his vest, and ere Paul Rayland could step aside, the fatal bullet passed through his heart, and the wretched culprit fell dead upon the grave of her he had loved but to betray! With a laugh of triumph, Rob turned away to seek the thick covert of the wood, but his flight was intercepted by a party of men who were out in search of the fugitive, and being secured, he was immediately borne away to answer for the life which he had just sacrificed to his own feeling of revenge.

The news of Paul Rayland's fate was soon spread abroad, but there were few who regretted the death of one whose career had long rendered him the terror of the neighbourhood. Even Florence had by this time learned to regard him with feelings very different to those which she had once bestowed upon him, and in a short time afterwards she was induced to transfer her affections to Edward Cavendish, whose generous nature seemed well calculated to obliterate all recollection of the unworthy object of her former misplaced affection. All now seemed to promise a future life of felicity; her father had completely renounced his fatal predilection for play, and the same day which witnessed her union with Edward, saw also the nuptial rites celebrated between her sister and Stephen Harland.

THE END

www.ingramcontent.com/pod-product-compliance
Lightning Source LLC
Chambersburg PA
CBHW081212170626
46811CB00010B/3256